# WARNING

This book contains sexually explicit scenes and adult language. It may be considered offensive to some readers. This book is for sale to adults ONLY.

* * * * * * * * * * * * * * * * * * * *

Please store your files wisely where they cannot be accessed by underage readers.

ISBN-13: 978-1987863185
ISBN-10: 1987863186

Other Books by Carla Coxwell:

<u>Star Bright New Adult Romance Series</u> (This series follows "<u>Fifty Recipes For Disaster New Adult Romance Series</u>")

Torn between her feelings for her agent, Jon, and Rich, a charming bad boy who has ties in the movie industry, Jenny finds herself working through her own past to try to get a grip on her present. As she struggles to learn the lesson that in Hollywood not everyone is what they appear to be, Jenny tries to become a person that she can be proud of. Will she be able to find love and success in Hollywood? Or will she be dragged down by her past forever?

<u>Torrid Exposure New Adult Romance Series</u>

April is finished with school and ready to build a career. Coming from a well-to-do family, she has decided to reboot her life completely. With family scars too deep to mend, April craves a fresh start. But the past is harder to shake than April ever would have imagined. At the center of it all is Bennett, an old family friend who is the heir to a billionaire media mogul company. Bennett and April haven't been able to stand each other since they were kids. But as the world shifts, the two of them discover the past might be the key to their future.

<u>Devil's Advocate BBW MC New Adult Romance Series</u>

When Kristie comes home from college, the last thing she is expecting is her world to be turned upside down by the appearance of her step-brother, Gray. Gray is rash, impulsive and breaks the law. Kristie's mom asks if she can try to befriend Gray, in hopes to get him on the straight and narrow. The plan backfires, however, as Kristie finds herself falling for Gray. Is it possible he feels the same way? The connection between them threatens to tear down everything Kristie has ever held dear.

<u>Obsessed Bounty Hunter Romance Series</u>

Jacqui Schneider couldn't help it. Every time the memories of her family's brutal murder haunted her, she had to escape. The only thing that could replace her sorrow was sex...and lots of it. Depressed and with no goal in sight, Jacqui continued on with her self-deprecating lifestyle until it all changed one day. Uncle Max, an old family friend, appeared unannounced. Jacqui was astonished when Uncle Max revealed a secret to her about her father. From those few words, Jacqui's world turned completely upside down. She really didn't know her own father. In fact, she didn't even know much about Uncle Max, except that he visited them for a few days at a time over the years.

Get the latest update on new releases from the author at:

https://www.carlacoxwell.com/newsletter

This book is Part One of the "<u>Fifty Recipes For Disaster New Adult Romance Series</u>"

Book 1

Trying to win a competition for best chef is cut-throat business. Kiara Sands has just won the opportunity of a lifetime. When she arrives at Fission, she has no idea just how much her life is going to change. She's immediately introduced to Jenny Foster and Robbs Martin, her competitors in the cut throat competition. The only thing Kiara finds more distracting than Robbs' hateful attitude is the handsome executive chef, Paul Weston. It doesn't help matters that Paul is quite taken by Kiara, and showers her with more attention than he gives her competitors.

Book 2

Life in the Fission kitchen has become difficult for Chef Kiara Sands. While she tries to focus on her work, the rest of the employees pass their time gossiping about her boyfriend, Executive Chef Paul Weston. Paul isn't making things easy either. His time is consumed with rearranging things for the pending changes in his life. He is pushing most of his workload off on Kiara. Instead of an apprentice, Kiara is acting more like manager in the kitchen. As Kiara and Paul's relationship is tested, a new threat arrives in the form of celebrity chef James O'Toole.

v

Book 3

Chef Kiara Sands finally feels like she's getting her life back on track. She's arrived in New York City to start her dream job as apprentice to celebrity chef James O'Toole. But just as she settles into her new life, her past comes back to haunt her. Jenny, Paul, and Robbs have all arrived in the city and they each want something from her. Kiara is convinced that her life will be perfect if they would just leave her alone. What she doesn't realize is that an unknown force is working against her, not to ruin her perfect life, but to end her life completely.

Book 4

Kiara learns that her scholarship at *Le Cordon Bleu* has been revoked and no one will tell her why. Her almost boyfriend, Chase Abbott, promises to look into it for her… he also gives Kiara and Jenny a safe place to stay until the police capture Robbs. The attraction between Kiara and Chase rekindles the moment they're reunited but Kiara isn't ready to start a new relationship. The women struggle to put their lives back together and live with the constant fear that Robbs will return. Will the police catch Robbs before he hurts Kiara and Jenny again? Will Kiara finally let down her guard and give in to her feelings for Chase? Or will everything end in disaster?

A New Adult Romance Series

# Fifty Recipes For Disaster

## Book One

## By Carla Coxwell

Copyright Revelry Publishing 2015

# Table of Contents

# Chapter One

"**ALL RIGHT**, chefs, you have ninety seconds to get your food plated and presented. If your dish isn't ready, you will automatically be eliminated."

My cooking instructor, Chef Michelle Lee, walks through the room, examining our stations. My fellow cooking students and I are competing for the chance to enter another competition. The winner of today's cooking challenge will get the chance to compete for a full-time apprenticeship at Fission, one of Austin's hottest restaurants.

I'm not confident in many aspects of my life, but I know I dominate in the kitchen. I begin plating my dish just as Chef Lee approaches my station.

"Your food presents beautifully as usual, Kiara," she tells me with a smile. "If it tastes as good as it looks, you've got this in the bag," she adds with a soft whisper.

The instructors at *Le Cordon Bleu College of Culinary Arts* aren't supposed to show favoritism to their students, but Chef Lee keeps a soft spot for me. Along with being one of my teachers, she's also my faculty adviser, and she knows the unusual circumstances that brought me to the school.

"Time's up," she calls out to the class. "Place your finished plates on the head table."

I walk my plate to the front of the room and place it on top of the placard that holds my student ID number. My classmates follow suit… several of them glare at me after looking at my dish. I am delighted, knowing they're all both jealous and impressed I was able to execute a well-developed *Cioppino* within the given time frame. My rich seafood stew is accompanied by fresh sourdough loaves. I examine my classmates' dishes and feel my chances of winning are good.

"Clear away your stations," Chef Lee directs. "Chef Lawton will be here shortly to judge your plates, and I don't want any evidence of who made what on display when he arrives."

Chef Lawton is the *sous* chef at Fission and the judge of this stage of the apprenticeship competition. I clear my station quickly and then I take a seat at the front of the room. I want to be able to see Chef Lawton's expressions as he tastes each dish.

As I sit nervously in my chair, my classmates finish clearing their stations. I can tell everyone else is just as anxious as I am… we've received plenty of critiques from our instructors but this will be the first time a professional chef from a restaurant will be tasting our food. The door of the classroom opens and a tall man wearing a black chef's jacket enters the room.

"Chef Lawton, it's so lovely to see you," Chef Lee welcomes him. "I can't tell you how excited we are to participate in this competition."

"We're excited as well," Chef Lawton replies. "We're always looking for new, innovative chefs at Fission. I'm looking forward to tasting the dishes and welcoming one of your students into the final leg of the competition. I see that all of the plates are ready. If it's all right with you, I'll get started."

"Of course," Chef Lee agrees.

I try not to hold my breath as I watch Chef Lawton sample each of the plates. I feel encouraged when he reaches mine. Instead of sampling one bite and moving on, he holds the broth in his mouth for a moment, and then tastes each type of seafood in turn. The expression on his face tells me that my stew is perfect, and I say a silent prayer I haven't been out-cooked by any of my classmates.

"First off, I'd like to say this is an impressive display," the seasoned chef begins. "Everything on this table is up to par with the level of skill and talent I expect to see from second-year students. That being said, there is a clear winner. One chef not only executed a delicious dish, but also added a few subtle, original touches that showed innovation and creativity."

Adrenaline rushes through me as he moves to stand behind my dish. "Who created this *Cioppino*?" he asks.

I blush involuntarily as I raise my hand.

"And what is your name, Chef?"

"Kiara Sands," I reply, trying to mask the excitement in my voice.

"Well, Chef Sands, it's an honor to welcome you to the next stage of the competition. I look forward to tasting more of your food as the weeks progress. I am needed back at Fission, but Chef Lee will provide you with the details of your new position." He turns to the rest of the class. "To the rest of you, don't be discouraged. You all provided me with excellent dishes, and you have bright futures ahead of you."

"Thank you, Chef," the class responds in unison.

Chef Lawton makes a quick exit, and Chef Lee takes his place behind the head table. "Excellent work today, class. You're dismissed until tomorrow," she announces. My classmates gather their things and leave the room… I stay behind to talk to Chef Lee.

"Kiara, I'm so proud of you." She beams once we are alone. "As you know, there will be two other chefs competing with you at Fission. You're the only one who's been selected from *Le Cordon Bleu*, and I know you'll represent us well." She moves to her desk and pulls a large package from her bottom drawer. "Here is your apprenticeship packet. You'll receive your Fission jacket when you report for work tomorrow morning. If you have any questions, or just need someone to talk to, you know where to reach me."

"This seems like a wonderful dream, and part of me is afraid that I'll wake up any minute now," I confess.

Chef Lee gives me a maternal smile. "This is a dream, Kiara. It's *your* dream. And you're well on your way to achieving it."

<<◇>>

The information packet Chef Lee presented me with instructs me to be at Fission at 10:00 am. I check my dashboard clock as I pull into the parking lot… 9:40 am. I feel smug, knowing I'm probably the first of the three competitors to arrive. I check my makeup in the rear-view mirror before exiting my car.

Fission is housed in a modern brick building in East Austin, one of the city's burgeoning hipster areas. The area gives off a relaxed, laid-back vibe, but I know the kitchen of Fission will be anything but.

I push open the heavy, solid oak door and am greeted by a pixy-sized hostess with spiked, lavender hair.

"Table for one?" she asks me brightly.

"No," I reply nervously. "My name is Kiara Sands. I'm supposed to start work today."

"Oh! You're one of the newbies!" She says warmly. "I'm Megan. It's a pleasure to meet you. The other two are already here. I'll show you to their table."

*Damn it!* I'd been so sure I'd make the best impression by arriving first, and here I am, the last of the apprentices to report for our first day.

Megan seems to sense my disappointment. "Don't worry. Paul doesn't give a shit how early people show up. As long as you're here when you're scheduled, you'll be fine. And you haven't missed anything. The other two have just been sitting alone since they got here," she offers reassuringly.

"Thank you for that," I say half-heartedly. As I follow Megan through the restaurant, I'm struck by the eclectic, well-placed décor. All of the tables are made of the same polished oak as the front door. The water goblets on the tabletops are tinted in hues of blue, green, and rose… a selection of art from all around the world adorns the walls. The ambiance is on the right side of the fine line between cozy and overwhelming. The restaurant offers a large main dining room, with smaller, more private rooms on each side.

"This is a beautiful place," I say as Megan leads me toward the back of the main room.

"It is," she agrees. "Paul handled all of the decorating himself. He says that Austin is a melting pot, and he wants all of our customers to feel at home when they dine here."

I'm about to comment on how successfully that goal had been achieved when we arrive at a table occupied by a beautiful blonde woman and a swarthy man with sandy blond hair. A pot of coffee and three cups sit on the table.

"Kiara Sands, this is Jenny Foster and Robbs Martin," Megan introduces us. She checks her watch before speaking again. "It's a quarter to ten, so I imagine that Paul will be out shortly. I suggest you get fully caffeinated and enjoy this time off your feet. It will be the last one for today," she warns with a friendly, knowing tone.

I take a seat in the chair next to Jenny as Megan moves back to the hostess station. "It's a pleasure to meet you both," I offer.

"It's a pleasure to meet you too," Robbs replies. "Congratulations on making it this far in the competition. And I'd like to apologize right now for how thoroughly I'm going to kick both of your asses. This job is mine." He speaks with a blend of arrogance and sarcasm, and I can tell immediately that Robbs and I are not going to get along.

Personal relationships are something I struggle with. In my experience, there's no point in getting close to someone who will inevitably let you down. I prefer to keep my head down and focus on getting my job done. As Chef Lee said yesterday, I have a dream and I'm well on my way to achieving it. I'll be damned if I let Robbs or anyone else get in my way.

"Just ignore Robbs," Jenny advises me. "He thinks that he's God's gift to food... women too, probably." She giggles. "So Kiara, what's your story? Which campus were you plucked from?"

"I'm in my second year at *Le Cordon Bleu*," I answer with pride. In my opinion, *Le Cordon Bleu* is the best culinary school in the area—it's also the hardest to get in to. Jenny seems impressed by my background, but Robbs laughs and dismisses it immediately.

"The *Bleu* is all right, I guess," he snorts, "if you're happy being complacent and doing everything old-school."

"I wasn't aware that being classically trained is a bad thing," I reply shortly. "Tell me, what culinary Mecca do you hail from?"

"*Escoffier*," he answers with a cocky smile. "You know, where all of the innovative, cutting-edge people attend. Three of my instructors were nominated for the James Beard award. So like I said, no hard feelings, but I'm going to kick both of your asses. *Escoffier* specializes in farm-to-table cuisine, so I'm exactly the kind of chef Fission is looking for."

I dismiss his statement with a glare. While the *Auguste Escoffier School of Culinary Arts* is reputed for turning out fantastic chefs, in some culinary circles it's dismissed as a hipster college that prioritizes food trends over basic technique and skill.

I don't feel like debating the merits of my education with Robbs, so I turn to Jenny. "And where do you go?" I ask pleasantly.

"The Art Institute," she replies. "I'm still not positive that cooking is my life's passion. I wanted to go to a college that offers other programs, in case I decided to change my major."

"If you're not sure that you want to be a chef, then what the fuck are you doing here?" Robbs asks hotly. "You should give your spot to someone who knows that this is what they want."

Jenny's green eyes fill with both anger and embarrassment, and I can tell she's fumbling for a response.

"I don't agree with that at all," I say warmly. "What better way to find out if you enjoy working in a real kitchen, than by actually doing it?"

"That's exactly what my instructor said when I won this spot," Jenny says with a nod.

"I see how it's going to be," Robbs interjects with more sarcasm. "The two of you are going to band together in 'sisterhood' and gang up on me."

"That's not how it's going to be at all," a firm voice says from behind me. I turn to see one of the most attractive men I've ever laid my eyes on. He's tall, with broad shoulders, blue eyes, and sandy blond hair. He's also wearing a black chef's jacket, identical to the one Chef Lawton wore when he judged my dish. He holds eye contact with me for several moments before he speaks again.

"This competition will come down to one thing and one thing only... the quality of your food. Only one of you will be named my new apprentice, so ganging up on each other won't serve any purpose. I'm Paul Weston, and I'd like to welcome you to my restaurant." He extends his hand to me.

I respond with a firm handshake and a smile. "I'm Kiara Sands. Thank you for this opportunity."

"You're here because you deserve to be. No thanks are necessary," he assures me.

"Chef Weston, it's an honor to meet you," Jenny gushes as she shakes hands with the executive chef. "I'm Jenny Foster."

"It's nice to meet you, Jenny," he says before turning to Robbs. "And I'm assuming that you're Robert Martin?" he asks while extending his final handshake.

"Just Robbs, Chef Weston," he responds with an air of professionalism. "I admire your talent and your vision. I'm confident I'll be a strategic asset to you."

"That will be for me to decide, Robbs," Chef Weston replies curtly. "Thank you all for being on time. I'm going to start by going over the rules here at Fission, and then we'll tour the building." He signals Megan before taking the final seat at our table.

"First and foremost, while you are here, you will show nothing but absolute respect for the rest of my staff. I take much care in handpicking each and every person who works in this restaurant. If you find yourself doubting the ideas, techniques, or decisions my staff makes, assume *you* are wrong, not them. You will do what you're told, and you will do it quickly, with a positive attitude. Is that understood?"

The three of us nod in unison.

"Fantastic. Now, that being said, I am open to hearing your ideas and opinions. You will discuss those ideas and opinions with me, and only me. If I like what I hear, I'll address it with the rest of the staff. I believe you all met Patrick Lawton, my *sous* chef?"

We all nod again.

"In addition to Patrick, there are seven line chefs working in my kitchen. You will work with each of them in turn, and they will provide me with input on who deserves the apprenticeship."

I shift uncomfortably in my chair as Chef Weston speaks. While there are three of us at the table, it seems as if he's speaking only to me. His eyes remain fixed on mine, and his face reacts to my expressions. *It's because you're the only one who comes from The Bleu. He knows you come from the best training… that's why he's speaking directly to you.* I repeat this over and over in my mind, but there's still a small part of me that suspects Chef Weston is interested in more than my cooking skills. As I try to convince myself that those suspicions are unfounded, Chef Weston continues to speak.

"Fission is open seven days a week, you will work six. You will all work twelve to fourteen hours on Saturdays and Sundays. If that presents a problem for any of you, you should leave now."

"That's not a problem at all," Robbs replies pompously. "In fact, I could pull more hours if you need it, Chef Weston."

"That won't be necessary," Chef Weston replies dismissively. "But your statement brings us to another point of discussion. When we are in the kitchen, you are all to address me and the other staff as 'chef'. Outside of the kitchen, you're welcome to call me Paul. The other chefs and I will provide you with the same courtesy."

"Let me explain my vision behind Fission," Paul continues. "I've always been intrigued by the role food plays in different cultures. After graduating from culinary school, I spent three years traveling the world and learning about exotic ingredients and techniques. When I came home, I opened Fission as a way to showcase what I'd learned and show how those ingredients and techniques can be blended to create food that is both exotic and familiar. There are no rules in my kitchen regarding the types of cuisine you can blend and the types you cannot. I encourage you to use your imaginations and your talent to make the best dishes possible."

"This sounds like my dream job," Robbs interjects. "And I'd like you to know I'm highly skilled in executing farm-to-table menus. I know that's important in today's culinary atmosphere."

*God, will he ever stop bragging about himself?*

"Robbs, if you're as skilled and knowledgeable as you should be, then you already know the farm-to-table concept is nothing new," Paul answers impatiently. "In many areas of the world, all restaurants are 'farm to table' and families rely on their harvest to feed their customers. While I admire the American chefs who are utilizing that concept in the U.S., I refuse to limit myself and my staff in such a strict way. At Fission, we use as many locally sourced ingredients as possible. All of our beef, lamb, pork, and chicken come from farms in the surrounding area, as well as our seasonal produce. But exotic ingredients are imported from the countries that know how best to grow them. I'm sure a chef of your caliber understands that."

Listening to Paul take down Robbs relaxes me, and I'm comforted to know that the executive chef and I share the same attitude toward food.

"Of course, Paul," Robbs replies in a defeated tone. "This is your restaurant, and I respect your vision."

"Fantastic," Paul continues. "Now that we've covered the cuisine, let me describe what your next twelve weeks will be like. As already stated, you will each work six days a week. During each shift, you will either assist one of the line chefs or you will be assigned other tasks that will help me understand your talents, skills, and visions. Once a week, we will hold a cooking challenge with specific requirements. The winner of each challenge will have their dish featured as a weekend special. High volume, fast-paced kitchens aren't for everyone, so if at any time you feel overwhelmed, you may bow out of the competition. As you're each receiving college credit for your work here, anyone who chooses to bow out will be allowed to continue helping in the kitchen through the end of the semester. Any questions?"

The three of us shake our heads.

"Perfect. We open for lunch in thirty minutes. I'll give you a quick tour of the kitchen, and then your first shift will officially begin. Today you will be shadowing the wait staff."

Robbs appears disappointed by the announcement, while Jenny's face reflects the confusion I feel at the assignment.

"I know what you're thinking." Paul smiles. "This competition is for a spot in the kitchen, so why are you bothering with the servers? I feel too many chefs become complacent in the kitchen. The chef is rarely the person who takes heat from the customers when their order isn't to their liking. I've also witnessed many chefs who believe, unjustly, that their training and skills make them superior to the servers. That is not the case here. Each employee serves a specific purpose. We are a team, and each member of the team is vital to the restaurant's success. During your time here, you will learn to appreciate the roles of each and every one of my employees. Is that understood?" Paul asks the question to all of us but directs his gaze specifically at Robbs.

"Of course," Robbs answers tensely. I can tell the day isn't playing out the way he expected.

Paul rises from the table and the three of us do the same. We follow him through the swinging doors at the back of the room and enter the biggest kitchen I've ever seen. Viking ranges line both horizontal walls, while a line of butcher-block tables cuts the room in half. Five chefs work on the lunch specials, in anticipation of the crowd that's sure to descend at any moment.

"Each member of the kitchen staff works their own station, ovens, and stovetops," Paul explains as we walk to the back of the room. Three-fourths of the back wall is made of stainless steel, and I correctly assume it's the walk-in refrigerator. Paul opens the metal door and gestures inside. "The walk-in is to remain clean and organized at all times. The introductory packet provided by your instructor details the health department codes for food storage. You will be tested on those first thing tomorrow."

Paul shuts the metal door and moves to the wooden one that opens to the other quarter of the space. "This is the pantry," he informs us. "Like the walk-in, it is to remain organized at *all* times. I can't emphasize the importance of this enough. For service to run smoothly, everyone who works here needs to be able to open these doors and go straight to what they need."

"Understood, Chef," I respond.

"Yes, with your *Cordon Bleu* background, I expect you do," he replies with a warm look. Once again, he holds his gaze on me a little longer than necessary.

Robbs visibly tenses beside me. He clears his throat. "Chef, I was told we'd receive our jackets when we arrived this morning?" he asks in an obvious attempt to steer the subject away from my education.

"You will receive your jackets when I decide you've earned them, Chef," Paul answers firmly. He turns to face the rest of the kitchen. "Chefs, gather for just a moment please," he calls out.

There is a clamoring of noise as each of the chefs pull pans off of their stoves and place utensils to the side. They line up in front of us as if they are military officers reporting for inspection.

"Chefs, these are the new up and comers who will be competing for the apprenticeship spot." As Paul introduces us by name, I now feel as if I'm the one being inspected. "Chefs Robbs, Jenny, and Kiara, this is most of the team you'll be working with. They will now introduce themselves and describe their duties."

The portly, bald man standing to the far right takes one step forward. "Welcome to Fission. I'm Chef Michael, and I'm the Roast Chef. I also serve as Butcher. I hope to enjoy working with all of you."

Chef Michael steps back and is followed by Chef Cole the *saucier*, Chef Henry the seafood specialist, Chef Harrison the grill-master, and Chef Jacqueline the fry chef. They each greet us warmly, but with reservation, as if they're sizing us up to determine if we're worthy to be in their kitchen.

"Chef Patrick and his assistant, Chef Carlton, as well as Chef Claire, our *pâtissier*, will arrive for the evening shift," Paul explains. "You will meet them before you leave tonight. If there are no questions, I'll escort you to the server station, where you will receive your shadow assignments."

# Chapter Two

I sit alone at a small table in the back of Fission. This is my third day at the restaurant, and the first I'll be allowed to cook. It's Thursday morning, and the first challenge for the weekend special will start in half an hour.

I've discovered I like to come in early and enjoy a pot of coffee before work begins. It gives me time to settle in and feel comfortable in the restaurant I still find a bit intimidating. Over the past two days, I managed to follow all of Paul's instructions and complete the chores assigned to me with a happy disposition. Tuesday, I shadowed Kinley, the head-waitress. I made polite conversation with the customers, carried her trays, and filled her drink orders. When we arrived yesterday, Jenny, Robbs, and I were informed we would be the cleaning crew for the day. Jenny and I bussed tables, washed dishes, and cleaned the bathrooms, all the while maintaining a pleasant, cheerful attitude. Robbs begrudgingly completed the same tasks, letting everyone in the restaurant know by his attitude that he felt he was above doing the scut work.

I hope my positive attitude, especially compared to Robbs' petulant one, is the reason Paul seems drawn to me. Over the last two days, I caught him gazing in my direction several times. He even helped me clean the ladies' room yesterday. He said as the boss, he believes he should never ask an employee to do something he's not willing to do himself. While that's a wonderful philosophy, I still feel like there's more to the attention he's giving me than professional admiration.

As I sip my coffee, I wonder about today's cooking challenge. I am confident in my skills, but I haven't seen Jenny or Robbs cook yet. For all I know, they are better than I am. I check the time on my phone just as Jenny walks through the front door. She sees me sitting at the back table, grabs a coffee mug from behind the bar, and joins me.

"Good morning," she greets me brightly. "Are you ready for the challenge?"

"I hope so," I answer with a nervous grin. "Paul said these challenges will be specific. I wonder what we'll be doing today."

"I don't know. I must say, the way this competition is set up reminds me of all of those cooking shows on television. I keep expecting a cameraman to pop up any second."

"That's exactly what I think!" I agree with a laugh. "I admit, culinary reality TV is one of my few guilty pleasures. I watch all of them."

"Me too!" Jenny replies. "I'd love to be on one someday... or judge one."

"Maybe one day we'll do one together." I don't make friends easily, but I like Jenny. She seems kind, honest, and genuine.

"My parents would just die if I end up on television," Jenny says. "They're incredibly conservative. I was never allowed to watch anything but the public access channels. And even then, they had to approve each show before I watched it."

"That sounds rough," I respond uncomfortably. I know what's coming next, and I dread it.

"What are your parents like?" Jenny asks.

This is a common question, and one I never answer honestly. "They were great," I answer quickly. "But they passed away when I was sixteen. I've been on my own ever since."

"Oh, I'm so sorry to hear that," Jenny quickly replies. She can sense I am uncomfortable and pulls out her cell phone. "I'm going to take advantage of these last few minutes and study."

I know this is her way of giving me some space, and I appreciate it. One thing I said to Jenny was true. I've been on my own since I was sixteen years old. Everything else was a lie. My parents weren't the best people, and they aren't dead... at least, not that I know of. My earliest memories with them are happy ones, but everything changed when I was around nine years old. That's when my father, a once-successful salesman, lost his job at the company he'd been with for twenty years. Instead of picking himself up and finding a new job, my father drowned his depression in drugs and alcohol. And instead of putting her foot down or leaving him, my mother joined him in his addictions.

After their savings ran out, my parents started selling drugs to pay for their habits. Between my ninth and sixteenth birthday, we moved fourteen times. Each new place was smaller and dirtier than the last, and I was usually left to fend for myself. When I was sixteen, I arrived home from school one day to find my parents had moved without me. The note they left behind is still tucked away in a box in a far corner of one of my closets. *Dearest Kiara, You'll be better off without us. One day you'll understand.*

I have no siblings and both sets of my grandparents died before I was born—that note was the end of my family. I shamefully explained my situation to the landlord, and he let me stay in the apartment until I graduated from high school. I worked two jobs to pay the rent and utilities, and I've become quite adept at taking care of myself. I'm not ashamed of my past, but it's not something I like to talk about, and I'm relieved Jenny isn't pushing the subject.

"I hope we're not required to make a dessert," Jenny says from across the table. "I haven't mastered pastries yet."

"I doubt it," I assure her. "The winning dish is going to be one of the weekend specials, so I'm assuming we'll be doing entrees."

"I hope so." She sighs. "I admit, I'm nervous."

"I am too," I agree as I refill each of our coffee mugs.

"If I don't win, I hope you do," Jenny says. "Robbs is a total ass. I wish we could vote him off the island."

"That would make life easier," I reply. As we joke, Robbs walks in the front door. He sees us immediately and joins us at the table.

"Good morning, ladies," he says with an arrogant grin. "Are you ready for the first of those ass kickings I promised you?"

"Sure, Robbs." Jenny smirks. "Give it your best shot. At the end of the day, we'll know who's got what it takes to be here."

"Your trash talking could use some work, Jen." Robbs smirks.

"I'd prefer if you didn't call me Jen, Robert," Jenny retorts.

As they glare at each other, Paul emerges from the kitchen with a pile of black jackets over one arm.

"Good morning," he greets us. "I hope you're all well rested and ready to get to work. There are three open stations in the kitchen. Today's assignment is fairly straightforward. You will each get a full hour to prepare an entrée. You must incorporate Latin cuisine with any other cuisines of your choosing. You're also required to incorporate at least one wood-fired element in your dish. At the end of the hour, you must present five professionally plated portions. Any questions?"

"No," Jenny, Robbs, and I answer in unison.

"Great. I'll be moving around the stations watching you as you work. I'll be judging your techniques as well as your final product." He pulls the jackets off of his arm as he speaks. "Before we step into the kitchen, I thought you all might like one of these." He passes each of us a jacket adorned with the Fission logo and embroidered with our names. We pull them on eagerly, but there is no time to admire them… Paul turns and moves toward the kitchen, and we follow. I know the exact dish I want to make, and I'm raring to get started.

We step into the kitchen, and I see the three stations closest to the back of the room are cleared off for us.

"You'll get quick access to the pantry and walk-in," Paul explains. "Chef Harrison has the grill fired up and ready, and he will taste your dishes today. You will also taste each other's dishes, not as a judge, but so you know what you're up against. Your knives are located at your stations, and your time starts now."

Robbs and Jenny immediately rush to the walk-in, so I head for the pantry. I'm going to make green curry tamales, so I gather mesa, corn husks, curry paste, and an assortment of other Indian spices. I deposit my selections at my station and move to the now unoccupied walk-in. I grab a beautiful piece of lamb, and then return to my station to mix up my marinade. I want to use the grill twice, first to cook my meat and then to sear the outside of my finished tamales. I slice the lamb and toss it into the marinade before starting on my corn mixture.

The aromas of soy and ginger fill the air and I know at least one of my competitors is preparing an Asian-inspired dish. I'm tempted to peek at their progress, but I control the urge. It wouldn't be professional, and I can't spare the time to worry about what anyone else is doing. I finish my corn mixture and then spread it out across the corn husks. Paul comes to my station to observe and I do my best to pretend he isn't there, despite the fact my pulse races every time he looks at me.

"This is an interesting combination," he says, glancing toward my marinating lamb. "I can't wait to taste it."

"Yes, Chef," I respond without looking up.

He leaves my station, and I decide I need a fresh element for my plate. A glance at the clock tells me I need to get my lamb on the grill, and I do it quickly. Chef Harrison stands watch over the fire to ensure we don't sabotage each other, so I leave the lamb and head back to the walk-in. I consider doing a Mexican street corn with Indian spices, but decide that would be too much corn on one plate. Instead, I grab fresh spinach, tomatoes, and tomatillos. I return to my station and chop the produce. I toss half of the tomatoes and tomatillos into a food processor and add chili and spices. With a quick whirl, my dipping sauce is ready. I can smell my lamb, and I rush to the grill to turn it. The meat is seared perfectly, and I'm happy with the progression of my dish.

I return to my station just as Paul approaches again. "Your knife skills are excellent, Chef," he says with a wink.

My stomach flutters, and all I can do is nod. *This is all part of the game. He's just trying to throw you off balance. Concentrate on the work.*

I whisk up a quick vinaigrette with ginger, garlic, and a touch of black cumin. I retrieve my lamb from the grill, spread it evenly across the corn mixture, and then roll the tamales. Once I place them in the steamer, I return to the walk-in and grab a couple of kefir limes. I grate the zest into my vinaigrette, then slice them and add the juice. The salad is finished and the tamales are steaming, so I finally steal a moment to take in my surroundings.

Robbs is bent over his cutting board, painstakingly rolling out fresh tortillas. Jenny is standing over the grill, and Paul is next to her. They each let out a laugh, and I'm startled by how jealous I feel that Paul finds Jenny so damn amusing. He's your boss, I remind myself. Or at least, he will be, if everything goes right. And the only way to make that happen is to keep my head in the game.

"Fifteen minutes, ladies," Robbs calls out. "I hope you're ready for disappointment."

I turn toward Robbs' station and see he is sweating. I don't know if it's because of the heat in the kitchen or the stress of the competition, but I'm happy to see he's losing his composure a bit. I return to the pantry and select my plates. I grab kidney-shaped bowls for my salad to ensure the vinaigrette doesn't soak into the rest of my food. I return to the kitchen and gently poke one of the tamales. It feels firm, so I use tongs to retrieve them from the steamer basket.

I pause for a moment, trying to decide how I want to present my food. Traditionally, tamales are served in their husks, but that creates quite a mess for the diner, and if there's one thing I hate, it is trash on a plate. I decide to de-husk them, and do so carefully before transferring them to a platter. Paul approaches once more as I make my way to the grill.

"No husks?" he asks. "That's an interesting choice."

"Yes, Chef," I reply nervously. Damn it. I knew I should have left them on. To think, I'm going to be done in by fucking corn husks.

There's nothing I can do about it now, so I continue my dish as planned. I gently place the tamales onto the grill, careful to keep the corn casing intact. I cook them just long enough to get beautiful grill marks on each side, and then quickly return to my station. With four minutes left, I want my plates to be perfect. I transfer the dipping sauce into a squirt bottle and squeeze intricate starburst patterns onto the left side of each of my plates. I place the tamales on top of the sauce, careful to leave at least half of them on the dry portion of the plate. I portion the salad into the bowls, and then set them on the right side of the plates. A few moments after I finish drizzling the vinaigrette over the salad, Paul announces that our time is up.

"Leave your plates at your stations. We're returning to the table at the back of the main dining room," he instructs us. We follow him into the dining room and take our seats. Chef Harrison joins us, and a few moments later, Sydney and James, two of the lunch waiters, appear with our dishes.

"Chefs, before we sample the plates, I'd like you each to briefly describe your dishes," Paul instructs.

I'm not at all surprised when Robbs opens his mouth first. "I've prepared cumin-spiced chicken raviolis with a Parmesan butternut squash sauce," he announces. There's so much pride in his voice that one might believe he raised the chicken himself. But his plate is beautiful, and I despise him for it.

Jenny clears her throat. "My dish is a Korean short-rib taco, with a cabbage jicama slaw," she says quietly.

"And you made the tortillas yourself?" Paul asks.

"Of course." She blushes.

"I made my pasta from scratch," Robbs interrupts eagerly.

"Yes, I know," Paul responds patiently. "There's no premade pasta dough in the kitchen, but there are plenty of corn tortillas." He turns to me. "Kiara, tell us about your dish."

"I made green curry tamales," I say quickly, "with fresh salsa and an Indian-spiced salad."

Robbs snorts at the mention of my salad, and I know he feels that I took the easy way out.

"All right everyone, let's dig in," Paul directs.

We silently sample each of the dishes in turn. Robbs' sauce is well developed, but his pasta is undercooked. I know after one bite that his dish won't be featured on the weekend menu. Jenny's dish, however, is delicious, and mine turned out exactly as I'd hoped. Paul and Harrison seem to agree with me. They finish the tacos and tamales but leave Robbs' pasta practically untouched.

"Robbs, now that you've tasted all of the dishes, I'd like for you to tell me where you went wrong," says Paul.

"The pasta could use a few more minutes in the water," Robbs answers coldly. "But I believe the sauce and the chicken were well seasoned."

"They were well seasoned," Paul agrees. "But that doesn't matter. If one thing is wrong on the plate, the entire plate is ruined. You walked in today overconfident, and that led to being careless with your dish. I suggest you don't make that same mistake next week."

"Yes, Chef," Robbs replies bitterly.

Paul turns to Jenny and me. "Ladies, both of your dishes were exceptional, and I'd be happy to serve either of them to our customers. But this is a competition, and a winner must be chosen. Harrison and I are going to speak in the kitchen for a moment, and then I'll return with our decision."

Paul and Harrison rise from the table and disappear into the kitchen. Robbs, Jenny, and I exchange glances but before we can comment on the challenge, Megan appears at the table with a pitcher of cola and three glasses.

"I know it gets hot in the kitchen," she says cheerfully. "I thought you might be thirsty. How did it go?"

"One of the girls won," Robbs answers harshly. "Paul and Harrison are in the kitchen deciding which one has the best rack... I mean dish."

He's crossed the line. "Are you suggesting our breasts had something to do with our abilities to fully cook our food?" I sneer.

Jenny lets out an involuntary chuckle. "This whole time I thought my skills came from hard work and studying. If I'd known my boobs were doing all of the work, I could have saved a fortune in tuition."

"I know, right?" I agree. "Poor Robbs doesn't stand a chance against our wonder-breasts."

Megan, Jenny, and I giggle while Robbs fumes in his seat. He opens his mouth to retort, but the kitchen doors swing open again and Paul returns to our table.

"Ladies, this was much closer than we'd expected. You both prepared delicious food, so since this was a grilling challenge, we based our decision on who we felt best utilized the cooking method," he announces.

Excitement fills my body. I used the grill twice, so I feel certain that I won the challenge.

"Kiara," Paul continues, "your tamales were delicious, and Harrison and I both enjoyed the fact that you pulled the husks before serving. Leaving them for the diner to remove leads to greasy hands and unnecessary trash on the plate, and it was better to avoid both situations. However, we felt Jenny's barbecued short-ribs best represented the grill. The smokiness of your lamb was overshadowed by the curry, whereas Jenny's sauce served to enhance that smokiness."

Jenny beams, and I offer her a weak smile.

"Congratulations, Chef Foster," Paul says warmly. "As your dish will be featured on this weekend's menu, I need you to walk Chef Harrison through it. He will ensure all of the ingredients are stocked, and you will be assisting him for the next three days."

"Of course, Chef," Jenny answers. "Thank you so much."

Paul nods at her, and she rushes off to the kitchen to find Chef Harrison. "Robbs, as your dish was the least successful, I'd like for you to return to the kitchen and prepare a plate of fresh fettuccini. No sauce is necessary, but I need to be sure you can correctly execute homemade pasta. Once I'm satisfied with your results, you will be handling the prep work for tonight's dishes."

"Yes, Chef," Robbs replies with defeat. He, too, returns to the kitchen, leaving Paul and I alone at the table. I sit quietly, expecting to receive my assignment for the day. Instead, Paul reaches across the table and rests his hand on my forearm.

"Kiara, I want to emphasize that your dish was fantastic," he says warmly, his clear blue eyes steady on my face.

"Thank you, Chef," I reply with a blush.

"Please, Kiara, we're not in the kitchen. Call me Paul."

"Thank you, Paul," I correct myself nervously.

"I watched you carefully during the competition. You have excellent instincts and incredible skill. I think you're going to do very well here." He pauses. "Your tamales made me wish that we could award two winners, but, unfortunately, that's not the case. As your runner-up prize, I'd like to offer you the opportunity to choose the chef you'll be assisting over the weekend. Harrison is already taken, of course, but you can pick among the rest. The list includes me, as I practically live in the kitchen during the weekends," he finished with a suggestive smile.

With his thumb, he traces small circles on my arm and shivers of excitement rush through my body. I pull my arm away before my emotions get the best of me.

"Thank you so much for the opportunity, Paul," I begin. "I look forward to working with you directly, but I think it would be best if I assist Claire this weekend."

"That's an interesting choice," Paul answers with surprise. "May I ask why?"

"Desserts are my weakest area," I explain. "I'd like to watch Claire... learn her tricks and secrets. I feel that's where I need the most help."

"It's admirable that you're aware of your weaknesses. It's even more admirable that you're willing to admit them," says Paul, smiling. "One of your competitors would do well to follow that example."

"Oh, but Robbs doesn't have any weaknesses," I say jokingly. "He was just thrown off because he wasn't able to visit the chicken farm before his main ingredient was slaughtered."

Paul laughs. "You're probably right. The 'full experience' is what the farm-to-table hipsters preach about, isn't it? I admit I was hesitant to even include *Escoffier* in the initial stages of the competition. Like you and Jenny, I was classically trained. But Patrick convinced me to give each of the area's culinary schools a fair chance, and he was impressed by Robbs' initial dish. We'll just wait and see if he can keep up with you girls."

"We're going to give him a run for his money," I assure Paul.

"Yes, I expect you will," he replies with a sly grin. He stands up. "Claire doesn't come in for another couple of hours. You're going to have a long weekend. Because of the demanding brunch menu, Claire stays late on Fridays and Saturdays and comes back at six a.m. on Saturdays and Sundays. Take the rest of today off and practice basic dough recipes and pastry skills. You should also brush up on your pastry bag skills. Claire is sweet, but she doesn't have a lot of patience for teaching."

"Thank you Che—Paul." I stop myself from addressing him formally. "I'll see you tomorrow. If you haven't had a decent plate of pasta by then, I'll be happy to make you one," I add jokingly.

"Thanks, Kiara," he says. "I may hold you to that."

Paul disappears into the kitchen, and I decide to use the restroom before heading home. I am disappointed I lost the competition, but it's overshadowed by the exhilaration I feel after my talk with Paul. There is no longer any doubt in my mind that he is interested in me, and the thought of spending time with him outside of the restaurant is both thrilling and terrifying. I check my makeup in the mirror before locking myself into a stall. My nerves over today's challenge made it hard for me to sleep last night, and I'm looking forward to getting home and crawling back into my bed. I'm just about to exit the stall when I hear the restroom door open and two female voices fill the room. I can't tell who the voices belong to, and I don't want to interrupt their conversation. I decide to remain in the stall until they leave.

"Can I borrow that lip gloss?" the first voice asks.

"Sure, just let me dig it out of my bag," the second voice answers.

"So should we start placing bets on which one of the new girls he's going to fuck first?"

"Charlotte, you're terrible," the second voice scolds. "If anything, we should warn both of them. I'm sick and tired of watching him fuck and dump every woman who walks through the doors."

"His shit didn't work on either of us," Charlotte reminds her friend. "If either of those girls is stupid enough to fuck him, then they deserve what they get."

I feel guilty about eavesdropping, but the women's conversation intrigues me. I wonder who they're talking about, and Charlotte's next statement confirms my worst fears.

"You know, I wouldn't be surprised if one of those girls tries to fuck her way into the apprentice position. You know that's how Claire got the *pâtissier* position. Patrick told me that several more qualified people applied for the job. But Claire spent one night with Paul, and then the next day she was hired."

My heart sinks, and I feel like I'm going to be sick. Just a few moments ago, I was imagining myself falling in love with Paul. Now I am sure he is nothing but a player. *Shake it off. This is for the best. Getting involved with him would just be a distraction, and Jenny and Robbs would resent me for it anyway. I'm going to win this apprenticeship, and I'm going to do it without taking my clothes off.*

"Maybe he'll hire that Robbs guy," says the second voice. "They could be each other's wing men."

"Oh, Amy, be honest. You had your eyes on Robbs since he first walked through the door. You want Paul to hire him so you'll have someone to play with."

"A girl can dream," Amy replies with a giggle. "We'd better get back out there and see if any of our tables are set."

I hear the women leave the restroom, but I remain seated in my stall, absorbing what I just learned about Paul. I decide there are two things I need to do. First, I find a way to shoot down Paul's advances without jeopardizing my position in the competition. Second, I need to warn Jenny about his history as a player. With a new resolve, I leave the restroom and head for home.

# Chapter Three

"It doesn't surprise me at all that Paul is a player," Jenny insists. It is Saturday, and the two of us are taking a break between the lunch and dinner rushes at the restaurant. As Paul warned, I've already had a long weekend and it's only half over. This is the first chance to tell Jenny about the conversation I overheard in the restroom.

We sit at a small bistro table in the café down the street from Fission. We'd both agreed we needed a break from Robbs, Paul, and Fission in general.

"It's absolutely disgusting," I tell her. "I feel so awkward working with Claire after hearing how she got her job."

"Does it appear like she knows what she's doing? I can't imagine Paul would put a bad chef in his kitchen, even if she's good in bed."

"She seems perfectly capable," I reply. "And her food is delicious."

"Maybe the gossip is only half right," Jenny suggests. "Maybe she slept with him, but that may not be the reason she was hired. You know how gossip works. It's like a margarita… it should be taken with several grains of salt."

"I don't like salt with mine," I say with an upturned nose.

"Come to think of it, neither do I…" she says, "but the saying still applies. We just need to keep our heads down and focus on our jobs. No good ever comes from sleeping with coworkers anyway. That's not a lesson I need to learn twice."

I can tell Jenny is trying hard to be my friend, but I'm still not quite ready to let my guard down. I've had too many 'friends' who were decent enough at first, but bailed as soon as I let myself be vulnerable with them. When people hear about my past, they become closed off and treat me as if I'm damaged. And as friendly as Jenny seems, at the end of the day she's still my competition. The last thing I want to do is let her know where my weaknesses are.

"You're right," I tell her. "It shouldn't matter if Paul is a player or a saint. He's our boss, and becoming involved with him isn't an option."

Jenny shakes her head. "Chauvinists always assume successful women slept their way to the top. The last thing either of us should do is prove them right. To be honest, I don't care if you beat me or I beat you… as long as Robbs doesn't get the apprenticeship, I'll consider it a win."

"Agreed," I reply. We lift our coffee mugs and toast our mutual dislike of our male competitor. I take a long drink of my coffee and check the time. "The dinner rush will be starting soon. We'd better get back."

As we exit the café, Jenny loops her arm through mine and we walk back to Fission together.

"I can't fucking believe they picked Kiara," Robbs hisses harshly. The three competitors had just finished the second cooking challenge, and the winner was just announced.

"You're just pissed that you lost again," Jenny insists. "Really, Robbs... you need to lighten up. Quit being such an ass during the challenges and maybe Paul won't feel the need to shoot your dishes down."

"You tasted her sauce, Jenny. It was fucking *broken*! Last week my pasta was slightly underdone, and I had to make the bastard a fresh plate so he'd know I'm not incompetent. And today we both watched little *Miss Cordon Bleu's* sauce separate on our plates, and he made it the goddamn weekend special!"

Jenny furrows her brow. "You do have a point. I know my seafood plate was a flop, but your duck was delicious. And Kiara's sauce did break..."

"He's fucking her, I know he is," Robbs insists. "Or he's trying really hard to. The way he fawns over her all of the time is disgusting. 'What a lovely plate, Chef Kiara,' 'I'm so impressed by your work ethic, Chef Kiara,' 'Let me help you carry those plates, Chef Kiara.' They may as well go at it on the prep table. I'm telling you, Jenny, if she hasn't already opened her legs, she's going to. And then we'll be out on our asses."

"I don't think Kiara would do that," Jenny insists.

"And you formed that opinion because you know her so well?" Robbs snorts. "Aside from where she goes to school, what do we know about her at all?"

"I know as much about her as I know about you," Jenny answers defiantly.

"I'm an open book," Robbs replies. "Ask me anything you want, and I'll give you a straight answer. Then go talk to that brown-haired bitch and see if she does the same. I'm telling you, I'm not going to sit back and lose this job because the boss man wants a hot new piece of tail... and you shouldn't sit back and take this either. You're an amazing chef, Jenny, and you deserve to be recognized for that. Paul's barely spoken to you since you won last week's competition. Not to mention that you're much more attractive than Kiara. I'd think if Paul wanted in anyone's pants, it would be yours."

Jenny blushes. "Thank you... I think," she says. "But I'm still not sure you're right about Paul. I mean, if you are, then we should obviously do something about it... maybe report him to our instructors or something... but until I'm as convinced as you are, I'm not going to do or say anything about it."

"What if I find a way to show you that I'm right?" Robbs asks deviously.

"What are you planning on doing?" Jenny answers with a tone of suspicion.

"Nothing illegal, if that's what you're worried about," he assures her. "But I could create a situation... see how he responds. I don't have an exact plan worked out, but you'll know it when you see it."

"You're going to do something to make her look bad, aren't you?" Jenny asks. "You're bitching about the competition being unfair, and now you're talking about sabotage. What's fair about that?"

"I won't do anything to get her kicked out of the competition. But I'm going to prove that he's showing her favoritism. If I can do that, will you help me do something about it?"

Jenny considers his question for several moments before answering. "IF I see something that makes me believe that Paul is showing Kiara favoritism because of anything other than her food, then yes, I will help you put a stop to it," she says.

# Chapter Four

"Kiara, I'm glad you're here early," Paul says as he approaches my usual morning table.

"I take my coffee here in the morning," I explain. "What's up?"

Paul takes a seat at the table and pours coffee into the mug he had carried over with him. "Enrique called about ten minutes ago. His wife went into labor this morning, so he's going to be out for a week or so."

Enrique is in charge of the daily prep work. Paul already told Robbs, Jenny, and I that we will be covering for him after his baby is born, so I know where the conversation is heading.

"Kiara," Paul continues. "I know your dish is the special this weekend, but Cole and Harrison will be executing the majority of it. Since Enrique's leave is starting on our busiest day of the week, I'm hoping you won't mind handling today's prep. You possess the best knife skills, and you work the fastest," he says with that charming smile that makes me want to melt into my chair.

"Whatever you need, Paul," I answer quickly. "I'm flexible."

"Thanks, Kiara. I knew I could count on you. You know, flexibility is an important quality for an apprentice. That will serve you well in this competition."

"Thank you. I enjoy working here, and I'll do anything to earn a permanent place in the kitchen."

"Anything?" he asks with a sly smile.

"Anything, within reason," I answer with a blush.

"I'll keep that in mind." Paul stares at me intently, and I think that he wants to say something else. Before he can speak, I am startled by the sound of a voice clearing behind me. I turn and see Jenny standing with her arms crossed.

"Good morning," she says coldly.

"Good morning," I reply. "Are you all right?" Something is obviously bothering her.

"I'm great... just ready to get to work." She turns to Paul. "What is my assignment for today?" she asks impatiently.

"Well, as you came in second in yesterday's challenge, you get to pick the chef you will assist this weekend. I was just telling Kiara that Enrique's baby is on its way this morning. She'll be handling the prep work, so you're welcome to assist Cole or Harrison, if you'd like to practice your grilling or your sauce skills. Everyone else is available too, of course."

I can see on Jenny's face that she's insulted by the suggestion that she help with my dish. "I'd like to assist you this weekend, Paul," she answers quickly. "You're the best, and I'm here to learn from the best."

"That will be fine, Jenny," he says. "I need to take care of some administrative stuff before I put on my jacket. Why don't you sit down and enjoy a cup of coffee with Kiara? You should be well caffeinated if you're going to keep up with me."

"I can hold my own," Jenny says boldly, "but a cup of coffee sounds good."

"I'll bring you a mug," Paul offers as he stands. Jenny takes Paul's abandoned seat across from me, while he walks over to the bar and fetches a mug for her. He brings it over to the table. "We'll get started in about half an hour," he tells her before heading off to his office.

Jenny stares at me for a minute before speaking. "So, you two were pretty cozy when I got here," she says with an air of accusation.

"We were just talking about covering the prep work. He's getting us to all take turns with it," I explain.

"I thought you felt uncomfortable around him after what you heard in the bathroom last week. But you certainly didn't seem uncomfortable just now."

Her hostility confuses me, and I'm not quite sure how to handle it. "He's our boss, Jenny. I'll talk to him. And I'm starting to think that Amy and Charlotte were exaggerating about him being a ladies' man. Like you said, gossip has a way of taking on a life of its own. I think Paul is just a good guy. And he obviously cares about other chefs, or he'd have never started this competition in the first place," I observe.

"Well, I guess I'll see how much he cares first hand over the weekend," Jenny answers shortly.

"Jenny, I'm sorry I ever said anything to you about what I overheard. Talking about it puts us on the same level as Amy and Charlotte, and we have more important things to do than gossip."

"Uh huh," Jenny replies. "Kiara, I'm sorry for being cranky this morning. I didn't sleep well at all last night. I wasn't happy with my dish yesterday, and I'm still shocked that he awarded me second place. It got me wondering about Paul, and whether or not he's showing us favoritism because we're women."

I laugh. "If he's showing us favoritism over Robbs, it's because we're not pompous pricks."

"You may be right about that," Jenny says. We sit and drink our coffee in silence for a while, and then she speaks again. "I'm going to head into the kitchen. Call me a brownnoser if you like, but I want to get Paul's station set up for him."

"I wouldn't call that brown nosing," I assure her. "I'd call that being proactive. I still need to look over today's prep list. I'd better get in there too."

We clear away our table and then set off for the kitchen.

# Chapter Five

"Chef Kiara, we needed those stuffed hens ten minutes ago," Robbs calls out impatiently. I was covering the prep station for four hours, and I'm completely in the weeds. If I'd been thinking more clearly when I planned out my work, I'd have started with those damn hens. Instead, I started with the *mise en place* for everyone's assorted dishes.

"I'll get them to you in ten," I call out. I grab a deep, stainless steel container and set off for the kitchen to retrieve the hens. At least the stuffing is ready. I toss twenty Cornish hens into the container and head back to the prep station. The hens are heavy. I heave the container onto the edge of the station and watch in horror as my cutting board tumbles to the floor, along with most of my day's work.

"Shit!" I scream. Everyone in the kitchen is staring at me... I avert my eyes helplessly and try to fight back my tears.

"What the hell happened here, Chef?" Paul demands as he walks over to the prep station. "I asked you to cover this because I thought you could handle it! Why am I looking at hundreds of dollars of produce and meat lying on my kitchen floor?"

"I'm so sorry Chef," I stammer. "I was just putting the hens on the table... I don't know what happened... I somehow knocked the edge of the cutting board off the side of the table... when I went to set the hens down, everything just came crashing down around me."

"Pay attention to what you're doing!" Paul growls.

"I know, I know. I'm so sorry! I'll fix it, Chef," I insist. I drop to my knees and start picking up the mess I made.

"It's okay, Kiara," Paul says softly. "We're just going to prep as we go." He turns to the rest of the kitchen. "Chef Kiara made a mistake, and I think we all know what that feels like." He takes a deep breath, and I can tell he's trying to come up with a plan for how to deal with my mistake. "Here's what we're going to do," he announces. "We're going to eighty-six my dish tonight. I'll ask the servers to take it off the board. Chef Jenny and I will assist Chef Kiara, and we'll just prep as we go."

The announcement draws sneers from everyone in the room, and none are as hateful as Jenny's. I know she's pissed about helping to fix my mistake, but I don't care. I'm just relieved I wasn't fired.

"Thank you, Chefs," I say almost inaudibly.

Paul puts an arm around me and leans into my ear. "Mistakes happen, Kiara," he whispers gently. "Shake it off, and don't let it affect the rest of your night."

My emotions get the better of me, and I wrap my arms around Paul. He returns my embrace and holds me tightly. "It's okay," he assures me again as he pulls away. "We've got your back."

Jenny approaches the prep station, her arms loaded down with fresh produce.

"I'm so sorry, Jenny," I apologize as she deposits the food onto the cutting boards. "I know this is the last thing you wanted to do tonight."

"Just pay more attention to what you're doing next time," she snaps. "I'm here to learn from professional chefs, not to clean up your messes."

I know there's no point in saying anything else, so I grab a knife and get back to work.

"Are you ready to admit I was right?" Robbs asks Jenny with a satisfied look on his face.

"Yes," Jenny replies angrily. "I can't believe I had to spend the entire night helping that bitch redo her prep. And I can't *believe* the bastard hugged her! If you or I had done that, he'd have chewed us new assholes. But nooooo... poor little Kiara just made a mistake. WE need to help her."

"I'm sorry that what I did ruined your night, Jenny," Robbs says softly. "I didn't mean for you to get mixed up in things. And I know that sliding that board over the edge of the table was a dirty trick, but if she'd been paying attention to what she was doing, she would have noticed it before she ruined all that food."

Jenny nods. "I'm not pissed at you, Robbs," she assures him. "I'm pissed at Kiara... and Paul. If he wanted to help her, he should have done it on his own. He could have transferred me to any other chef in the kitchen."

"And you saw the way Kiara wrapped her arms around him, didn't you?" Robbs asks. "Do you still think she's only interested in him on a professional level?"

Jenny shakes her head. "I overheard them this morning. I didn't have a chance to tell you about it yet, but Kiara told Paul that she's willing to do *anything* to win the apprenticeship. And believe me, when he heard that, he was damn near drooling. It was disgusting."

"Does she know you heard them?"

"Yep. And I made it pretty clear that I thought she was being shady. She insisted they were just talking about work. But she also made it pretty clear that she thinks Paul is a decent guy. It's only a matter of time before they start hooking up. You and I could out cook Julia Child and still not win this contest."

"How far are you willing to go to keep that from happening?" Robbs asks quietly.

"As far as it takes," Jenny answers with determination.

<<◇>>

"I enjoyed working with you this weekend," Jenny tells Paul. "Especially today, when we actually got to cook together... your tenderloin was divine."

"I enjoyed it as well," Paul replies politely. "I was impressed by the way you handled yourself in the kitchen, and the credit for the tenderloin belongs more to you than me. Your skills at the roasting station are phenomenal. I may get you to assist Michael next weekend."

"Unless I win Thursday's challenge," she reminds him with a grin.

"Yes, of course," he says. "If you win Thursday's challenge, you'll execute your own dish next weekend."

It's nearly midnight, and the wait-staff have already left for the night. Paul, Jenny, Robbs, and Claire are the only chefs still in the kitchen. Paul and Jenny are cleaning the roasting station, while Claire and Robbs finish wiping down the butcher-block tables.

"Chef, I'm just about finished up for the night," Claire calls from across the room. "The muffin batter is ready. I'm going to wait until morning to bake them off."

"Great, Claire, good work tonight... drive home safely," Paul replies. "Robbs, if you're finished, you can go ahead and leave too. Jenny and I will do a bit more scrubbing, but we're not far behind you."

He turns to Jenny as the other two chefs exit the kitchen. "You can go ahead and leave too, if you'd like," he offers.

"Actually..." Jenny begins slowly. "I was hoping you can help me with something. I'm taking a class next semester on pairings... you know, alcohol and food?"

"Yes, Jenny, I know what pairings mean," Paul says with an indulgent smile.

"Of course you do," she says with a forced blush. "I don't have a good understanding of the process, and I was hoping you might be able to give me some tips. I know it's late... and you probably don't feel like drinking..."

"As it happens, I'm quite skilled at pairings," Paul tells her with a cocky grin. "And I'd be happy to give you a few pointers. If you'll finish up here, I'll hit the walk-in and the bar and set up a tasting area."

"Thank you so much!" Jenny gushes. "I know I'll be a shoe in to ace the class if a chef of your caliber shows me the ropes first."

"You're more than welcome, Jenny," Paul replies. "I'm always happy to help the next generation of chefs. That's the whole point of this competition."

Paul carries a large tray into the walk-in while Jenny continues scrubbing the roasting station. As she finishes up, Paul reappears with an assortment of cheeses, produce, and cold cuts.

"We'll start off simple," he explains as he gestures to the platter in his hand. "It'll be easier to do this at the bar."

Jenny carries her rag to the sink, rinses it, and follows Paul through the swinging kitchen doors.

"Thank you for asking me to do this," Paul says as he sets the platter down and steps behind the bar. "I need to teach all three of you about pairings. We always offer drink suggestions alongside our menu items, but I forgot all about having you guys sample them."

"I'm excited to learn." Jenny beams. "I know the basic pairings. You know... champagne with strawberries... white wine with fish, red with beef. But that's where my knowledge ends."

"Well, why don't you take a bite of a strawberry and then a drink of this?" Paul suggests. He holds out a glass of white wine and Jenny accepts it.

"That's amazing!" Jenny says after sampling the pairing. "After tasting the strawberry, the berry flavor in the wine just pops!"

"Take another sip and tell me what else you taste," Paul directs.

Jenny complies. "Hmmm... peaches, green apple... and pepper?"

"Impressive," Paul replies. "You're better at this than you think." He slices a thin piece of sharp cheddar and pours a splash of red wine into a glass. Jenny reaches for them, but he quickly stops her.

"You need to cleanse your palate between wines," he explains. He grabs a bottle of Kettle One vodka and pours them each a shot.

"You're right, that does help," Jenny tells him after downing her shot. She samples the cheese and red wine together. "The crispness of the wine is a welcome contrast to the creaminess of the cheese," she observes.

Paul pours them each another shot of vodka before pairing prosciutto with a light chardonnay. They continue the process for an hour, with each of them taking a shot between samples.

"I'd like to work on beer pairings next, but I'm afraid I'm already pretty drunk," Jenny teases. She rests her chest on the bar and positions her cleavage directly in Paul's line of vision. He tries not to stare, but he can't help himself.

"We can do beer pairings another night," he suggests. "And next time, we'll use black coffee to cleanse our palates," he adds.

"I know I already thanked you, but I hope you know how much I appreciate this, Paul," Jenny says, dropping her voice to a seductive tone. "I admire you so much." She reaches across the bar and places a hand on top of his. He flinches at first, then opens his fist and caresses her hand with his forefinger.

"Thank you, Jenny. It's always nice to hear that I'm appreciated."

Jenny stares into his eyes. "You know, I'm no expert, but there's always one thing I enjoyed with my alcohol," she says daringly.

He holds eye contact with her as she wraps her hand around one of his fingers and begins stroking it up and down. "Oh yeah? What's that?"

"Sex," she answers boldly.

"Jenny... I don't know if that's the best idea. We work together... I'm your superior." He breathes heavily as she continues stroking his finger.

"I don't see why that matters," she whispers. "I'm not talking about a relationship. Just two people enjoying each other after a long day at work." She rises from her stool and climbs on to the bar, still stroking Paul's finger with her soft hand. "Would that be such a bad thing?"

"Well, when you put it that way," Paul says. "How is a guy to resist?" He wraps her hair in his free hand and pulls her lips to his. They kiss passionately, and Paul climbs onto the bar next to Jenny. "No strings attached?" he says quietly as he pulls her shirt over her head.

"No strings attached," she assures him as her honey blonde hair falls over her shoulders. She wiggles out of her pants while Paul strips off his clothes.

"Do you want to move to a booth?" Paul suggests. "It may be more comfortable."

"I'm fine here," Jenny insists. "I want you to fuck me on this bar, so you'll think of me every time you see it."

"As you wish," Paul replies. He pulls a condom from the pocket of his discarded jeans, opens it, and rolls it over his long, thick cock. He pushes Jenny's legs apart and buries himself inside her.

"Oh, Paul," Jenny moans as he rocks in and out of her. "You feel so amazing." She clenches her pussy muscles around him as he leans down and takes one of her breasts into his mouth.

"You feel pretty amazing yourself," he tells her.

Jenny arches her back, giving him easier access to her erect nipples. "Bite me, lover," she demands.

Paul does as he's told, nibbling each breast in turn as the juices of her satisfaction flow over his cock.

"You like that?" he says gruffly. "Are you coming for me, baby?"

"Yes!" Jenny cries out. "So hard... keep giving it to me, Paul."

Paul jackhammers into her. He isn't ready to come, but he's too drunk to stop himself. "I'm going to come with you, baby," he moans.

"No!" Jenny moans. "Don't stop. I want you to fuck me all night long."

Paul tries to hold back his orgasm, but he loses all control of himself. He explodes in ecstasy and collapses on top of her.

"I'm sorry," he says after a few minutes. "I couldn't stop myself."

"That's all right," Jenny assures him. "That just means you'll have to make it up to me, some other time."

Paul hops off of the bar and helps Jenny to the floor. They dress quietly, and neither of them notices Robbs lurking on the other side of the restaurant.

"Can I call you a cab?" Paul offers.

Jenny shakes her head. "My apartment is only a few blocks away. I walk to work."

"This is a pleasant neighborhood," Paul observes. "How do you afford a place here?"

"We all have our secrets," says Jenny. "I'll see you in the morning?"

"I'll be here." Paul walks Jenny to the door and locks up behind her.

Outside, Jenny reaches into her purse and retrieves her phone. She scrolls down to Robbs' number and calls it.

"Did you get it?" she asks.

"Every last second of it," he tells her. "That was quite a show. I can't wait to play the video for Kiara."

"Just hold on to it for now," Jenny insists. "This is too good to waste. We'll keep our eyes and ears open for the right time to strike."

# Chapter Six

"Jenny, are you sure you're all right?" I ask as we clean our stations after the lunch rush. A week has passed since my supreme fuck up at the prep station, and Jenny has been distant with me ever since.

"I'm fine," she insists. "I'm just tired. And I'm frustrated that Robbs won this week. It's only Friday afternoon, and I'm already about to choke on all of his smugness."

"I understand," I assure her, but I don't think she's being completely honest with me. Something strange is going on at Fission. Paul is still shamelessly flirting with me, but he's softened his attitude toward Robbs. And he's been downright short with Jenny. She came in last in this week's competition, even though her lobster was decadent and my prawns were overcooked.

"I'm a little tired myself," I tell her. "Want to walk down to the café with me over our break? I could use a shot of espresso... or five."

"A strong cup of coffee does sound good," she agrees.

We walk into the employee break room to retrieve our purses and find Amy and Charlotte laughing at the table. They silence themselves abruptly when they see us in the doorway, and I see Charlotte shoot Jenny a dirty look.

"Hi, girls," I say kindly, breaking the silence. "We're going to walk to the café for lunch. Would either of you care to join us?"

"No thanks. Our break is almost over," Amy answers for both of them.

Jenny grabs both of our purses and pushes me back through the door.

"What do you think that was about?" I ask.

"Who the hell knows with those two?" Jenny says. "They're probably just talking shit. I swear half of the people in this place act like they're still in high school."

"God, I hated high school," I groan.

"Really?" Jenny asks in surprise. "I thought you'd be in the popular crowd. You have the body of a cheerleader," she says with a tone of resentment.

"Nope," I say, shaking my head. "I was kind of a loner. I never was good with other people... I always preferred to keep my head down and work."

"So you were in the smart group? Hours and hours of studying?"

"Not exactly," I say. I don't feel like revealing my entire past, but I'm compelled to give Jenny a few details, if for no other reason than to get rid of the jealousy she's directing at me. "I worked two jobs while I was in high school. Once my parents were gone, there was no one left to take care of me, so I had to make sure my bills were paid."

"Oh God, Kiara, I didn't realize that," Jenny says apologetically. "Didn't your parents keep life insurance?"

"No, they weren't big on planning for the future. I lost them so unexpectedly. It actually helped to throw myself into work. I was too busy to think about them."

We step into the café and place our orders at the counter. "Want to share a club sandwich?" I ask.

Jenny shakes her head. "I don't have much of an appetite."

She pays for her latte, and I order a macchiato and a slice of vegetarian quiche. We make our way to a small booth and sit down before continuing our conversation.

"Jenny, are you sure you're all right?" I ask again. "If you don't want to talk about it, I completely understand, but you seem a little off this week."

"I was just questioning my decision to compete for the apprenticeship," she confesses.

"But you're so talented!" I argue. "Why would you question yourself? I know that when we started, you weren't sure that being a chef is what you want. Did you find something else you're interested in?"

"No... but, Kiara, you can't tell me you didn't notice the way Paul's been treating me lately," she says softly.

"I did notice," I tell her. "Did something happen? Did he make a pass at you? Oh god, what Amy and Charlotte said that day is true, isn't it?"

Jenny hesitates before answering. "It's nothing like that. I'm just afraid that he's realized I don't belong here... not like you and Robbs."

A waitress arrives with our orders, and we sit quietly until she leaves.

"That's ridiculous," I tell her. "It would be one thing if you'd decided to change your major. But you're incredibly talented, and you deserve to be here. Even more of a right than Robbs, because you're not a douchebag."

Jenny doesn't find my joke funny, which surprises me. Since our first day at Fission, we've bonded over our mutual dislike of Robbs. "Robbs isn't a bad guy," she argues. "He's cocky, but most talented chefs are. And part of his attitude comes from the fact that Paul shows you such obvious favoritism."

*Ahh, so that's the problem.*

"What favoritism?" I ask with frustration. "Robbs won yesterday, didn't he?"

"Yes..." Jenny agrees. "But you're the only one of us that Paul's nice to. He flirts with you all of the time, Kiara."

"But it's harmless, and I don't reciprocate," I argue. "Is that why you've been so distant toward me lately? Do you think I have something going on with our BOSS? You know I'd never do that! We talked about it the first time we came here!"

"I don't know what you would or wouldn't do, Kiara," Jenny hisses. "But I'm certain that Paul would take you in a second, if he thought he could."

"He *flirts* with me, that's *all*," I insist. "What do you expect me to do about it?"

Jenny slams her coffee cup down on the table, slides out of the booth, and grabs her purse. "Nothing, Kiara," she says hatefully. "I don't expect you to do a goddamn thing."

She rushes out the door, leaving me alone at the booth.

"You've done a fantastic job today, Kiara," Paul says. "You know, your work ethic is better than any of my employees. I love the way you keep your head down and focus on the tasks at hand."

"Thank you, Chef," I reply shortly. Two days have passed since Jenny and I fought at the café, and she's barely spoken to me since. Paul hasn't noticed the tension between us, but Robbs certainly has. He and Jenny started drinking their coffee together in the mornings and disappearing with each other during our lunch breaks. I catch them sneering at me but pretend not to notice.

"Listen, Enrique was supposed to stay late and clean up tonight, but his baby is colicky and his wife's exhausted. I'd like to let him off early, if you don't mind staying."

"Whatever you need, Chef," I agree.

The restaurant is slow for a Sunday, and three of the chefs were sent home. I spend the rest of the day manning the fry station, while Jenny and Robbs work together on Robbs' scallop kabobs, the dish that won him the latest cooking challenge. I hear them whisper as I work, and I know they're talking about me. Their attitudes make me even more sure of my decision to keep my past a secret from them.

The kitchen closes at eight o'clock on Sundays, and by quarter after, Paul and I are the only ones left in the kitchen.

"I'm going to supervise the front of the house cleanup, if you can get started on the ovens," Paul announces.

"No problem," I agree. I welcome the silence and the solitude. I know Jenny and Robbs are off somewhere talking about the fact that Paul and I are working alone in the kitchen tonight, but I don't care. Fuck them. Robbs is jealous because I'm a better chef than he is. Jenny is jealous of that too, *and* the fact that Paul finds me attractive. She probably just wants him for herself. Hot blondes like her always think they can have any man they want. She probably made a pass at him and got shot down. That would explain why he's been so distant with her... and why the waitresses keep giving her those dirty looks.

"How's it going in here?" Paul's voice startles me. I turn to see that he's just walked in to the kitchen.

"Good," I tell him. "Three ovens are cleaned, with two to go. Then I'll start on the stovetops." My stomach growls loudly as I speak.

"My goodness, Kiara. Have you eaten today?" Paul asks.

"I forgot," I confess with a blush. The truth is that Jenny and Robbs' attitudes had made me lose my appetite.

"Well, we're in the perfect place to do something about that," Paul says. "What sounds good?"

"I'll just eat whatever's left over from dinner service," I answer quickly. "I don't want to make a mess or be any trouble."

"That's ridiculous, Kiara!" Paul insists. "You have a world-renowned chef offering to prepare you whatever you want! You should take advantage. Opportunities like this don't come around every day." He smiles. "What is your absolute favorite thing to eat?"

"*Croque Madame*," I answer sheepishly. "I know it's not fancy, but it's what I like."

"That's one of my favorites too!" Paul exclaims with a broad grin.

"I can work on the béchamel sauce, if you want to grill the sandwiches," I offer.

Paul shakes his head. "You've been working your ass off all day. I'll handle everything." He disappears through the kitchen doors and returns a moment later with a bottle of chilled Zinfandel and two glasses. He pulls a stool over to one of the butcher-block tables and gestures for me to take a seat.

"I'm going to have a glass of wine," he says. "Would you like to join me?" I recognize the brand name and know that the cost of the bottle would cover my electric bill twice.

"I'd love one, thank you," I accept graciously.

Paul pours the wine, then sets off for the walk-in. He emerges with a tray of smoked ham, gruyere, butter, eggs, and cream. "Claire made some *Challah* this morning. Does that sound good to you?"

"*Challah* always sounds good." A warm, relaxed feeling fills my body as I finish my first glass of wine. "Do you mind if I pour another?" I inquire softly.

"Of course not. Pour as much as you like."

"You know," I say as I pour the wine, "I don't usually drink anything this expensive."

Paul laughs. "I remember being a poor college student. Until I opened the restaurant, I never drank the expensive stuff either. The only reason we're drinking it now is because I can write it off."

"The perks of being the boss," I say with a grin.

Paul fires two burners and sets small skillets on top of them to warm. He slices the beautiful loaf of *Challah*, butters one side of each piece, and assembles the sandwiches in the skillets. He fires a third burner, retrieves a saucepan from the rack, and starts on the sauce.

"This is one of the first things I ever learned to make," he tells me. "Well, sort of. Back then, it was just a grilled ham and cheese with Rotel sauce."

"That doesn't sound half bad," I tell him.

"Back then it was delicious," he agrees. "But today, you won't catch me dead near a block of Velveeta."

"Grilled cheese was one of the first things I learned how to make too," I confess. "But I rarely had any ham to add."

"I thought so," Paul says, nodding.

"You thought what?" I ask in confusion.

"That you grew up poor... no, no, I didn't mean that in a bad way," he says quickly when he sees me blush. "I grew up poor too. My father left my mother before I was born. She worked three jobs to make sure my sister and I didn't go without anything we needed. But there wasn't much left over for the things we wanted..." He flips the sandwiches in the skillets. "I was the oldest, so a lot of the cooking and housework fell on me. That's how I learned about fusing different flavors. We were all tired of eating the same stuff over and over again, so I started experimenting. I fell in love with cooking… it was my way of taking care of my family."

I finish my second glass of wine and pour the third as I reply. "I started cooking out of necessity. You're right, I grew up poor. But I didn't have anyone working to take care of me. Both of my parents were alcoholics and addicts. If I hadn't learned to cook, I'd have starved to death."

"You said your parents were addicts... have they recovered?" Paul asks gently.

I can't believe I'm opening up to him, but something about the way he's looking at me makes me feel safe. "I wouldn't know," I answer plainly. "When I was sixteen, I came home from school and they'd moved without me." I tell him about the note that's still hidden away in my closet as he plates the sandwiches, drenches them in sauce, and gingerly lays the fried egg on top.

"I can't imagine what that must have been like for you," he says softly. "Why in the world did you save that note? I'd think that it would be a painful reminder."

"It is," I agree with a nod. "But it also makes me grateful. My life has been far from perfect, but things started looking up for me once I was on my own. It was difficult, of course, keeping a roof over my head and keeping my grades up at the same time. But I shudder to think of where I'd have ended up if my parents had stuck around."

"Wait, you were completely on your own?" he asks in awe. "No aunts or grandparents to help you?"

"No one," I answer sadly. "My grandparents were gone before I was born, and my parents burned every bridge they had during their downward spiral."

"And you were too proud to ask for help," Paul guesses.

"What makes you think that?" I ask.

"The way you carry yourself... the determination you show in the kitchen. It says a lot about your character."

"Thank you, I think," I say, smiling. With a large fork, I pierce the egg and let the yolk gush over the rest of my sandwich. The first bite is heavenly. "This is the most delicious thing I've ever put in my mouth."

"You're just hungry," Paul insists. "I can do much better. Wait until you taste my empanadas."

"So, you're planning on cooking for me again?" I ask.

"I'll cook for you whenever you like," he answers seriously. He's looking at me again, in that way that makes me feel like he's imagining our future together. Suddenly I'm reminded of the hostility I've been getting from my fellow competitors. Emboldened by the wine, I decided to bring up the issue.

"You know, I'm pretty sure Jenny and Robbs have been gossiping about us," I tell him.

"They have?" I can tell that he's not surprised. "What are they saying?"

"I haven't heard anything directly from Robbs, but I know Jenny thinks you've been showing me favoritism... because you're attracted to me."

"Well, Jenny is absolutely right, and absolutely wrong," he says firmly.

"I don't understand. What do you mean?" I ask with a wine-induced giggle.

"I am attracted to you, and you are my favorite. But you're not my favorite *because* I'm attracted to you. You're my favorite because you're the most talented competitor."

"Do you really think so?" I ask. "I only won one of the challenges, and you and I both know the sauce was broken."

"The flavors of that dish were perfect," he says quickly. "And I wouldn't expect a perfect sauce from a second-year culinary student. *Sauciers* spend years perfecting their craft. Ask Cole, if you don't believe me. I do, however, expect second-year students to be able to cook a plate of pasta, which Robbs did not."

"If a man had served you the dishes I prepared, would you think he was the best?" I ask with suspicion.

"You've been listening to the gossip around here," Paul answers with a grin. "Kiara, I made mistakes. I got involved with people I shouldn't have, and some of what you heard about me is probably true. But I'm serious about who I put in my kitchen, and you're the best chef I've seen in years. And, yes, I'd feel the same way if you were a man."

"Thank you," I say with a sigh of relief. We sit silently for several minutes enjoying the food in front of us. "That was delicious," I tell him as I push my empty plate away.

"Thanks," he responds. "I look forward to cooking for you again."

"Paul..." I begin slowly, "a few minutes ago, you mentioned getting involved with people that you shouldn't have. I'm one of three people competing to be your apprentice. Am I not the definition of 'people you shouldn't get involved with'?"

"Yes," he says. "But that doesn't stop me from wanting to be involved with you."

"But it will never be the right time," I argue. "It would be inappropriate now. And if I win the apprenticeship, which I plan on doing, it will be inappropriate then, too."

"Are you attracted to me, Kiara?" he asks. I blush and remain silent. "Come on now," he encourages me, "I laid out all of my cards on the table. You know how I feel. So tell me, do you find me attractive?"

"Of course I do," I confess.

"Do you have many friends, Kiara?" he asks softly.

Again, I feel compelled to be honest with him. "No, I don't have any friends. I thought Jenny and I were getting close, but then something changed."

"So what would the harm be if we spend some time together, just as friends?" he asks. "This may come as a shock to you, but I don't have many friends either... I have employees. But when I'm away from the restaurant, I'm either alone or babysitting my sister's kids. I think it would be a welcome change to be away from here and enjoy some adult conversation."

"Just as friends?" I ask hesitantly.

"Just as friends," he assures me.

"I guess there'd be no harm in that."

"Perfect." He smiles. "Would you like to meet me for dinner tomorrow night? It's your day off, and I know a great little hole in the wall Thai place. Then maybe we could get some coffee after and just talk."

"I'd love to," I answer.

# Chapter Seven

I walk through the parking lot of Barton Creek Square, digging for my keys in my purse. I find them at the bottom and push the alert button on my keyless entry remote. I hear the horn of my car blare in the distance and start walking toward the noise. As I walk, I realize that I'd left the mall from a different set of doors than I'd entered. That explains why I lost the damn car. I am filled with relief when I finally set eyes on my twelve-year-old Honda Civic. I climb in and toss my bags in the seat beside me.

Initially, I'd planned on buying a new top to wear for my evening with Paul. But I'd given in to temptation, and with encouragement from a perky sales clerk, I'd purchased an entire outfit, shoes and all. I pull my new emerald green top from its bag, hold it to my face, and study myself in my rear view mirror. As I hoped, the shade of the fabric complements my skin in the natural light as well as it had under those god awful fluorescents.

Suddenly I am overcome with sadness. When I was a little girl, my mother always dressed me in emerald green. "It blends in so beautifully with your dark eyes and hair," she'd always say. I toss the shirt back into the bag and shake off the onslaught of emotions. So she knew what color to dress me in. That doesn't make her a good mother. I'm not missing out on anything, living my life without her.

I pull out of the parking lot and turn right, mindlessly driving toward my apartment. I scold myself for getting emotional over the mother who left me. This always happens before I go out on a date with someone new. I start wondering what my mother would say if she was here. What advice would she give me? Would she curl my hair and tell me stories of the dates she went on when she was my age? I'll never know, so I may as well stop torturing myself.

With no memory of the drive, I pull into my apartment building. It's a small, charming place in an area that was once the trendiest neighborhood in Austin. The crowds have long since moved on, but the buildings have been well maintained and the neighborhood is still safe. Most importantly, there are no drug dealers in my building. I can spot a dealer from a mile away. I know someone on my floor smokes weed because I sometimes smell it in the hallway, but that doesn't bother me. Hell, I toke up myself sometimes when life gets overwhelming.

I ride the elevator to the third floor, unlock my door, and step into my cozy home. My furniture is a collection of thrift store finds that I refinished myself, and my walls are covered in bright, abstract floral paintings. I toss my bags onto the sofa and walk to the bathroom. I need a long, hot shower before I get ready for dinner.

I get the water to the perfect temperature, slink out of my clothes, and step into the tub. The warm water rushes over me, washing away the hurt I feel after thinking about my parents. I decided to focus on the future instead. I let myself fantasize about Paul. As I wash my hair, I imagine us going to the farmers' market on our days off and cooking delicious food together in my kitchen. I wonder what his lips would feel like, pressed against mine, and remember the soft touch of his hand.

Thinking about Paul in this way turns me on, and I decide to indulge myself. I take my handheld shower head from its cradle and sit down in the tub. I lay back, switch the water stream to massage mode, and point it at my clit. As the water dances over me, I imagine it's Paul's tongue providing the sensations. I pinch my nipples with my free hand and soon I'm rewarded with a soft, satisfying orgasm.

Better safe than sorry, I think as I stand back up. I reach for my razor and quickly shave my legs. Satisfied that I'm well groomed, I turn off the water, step out of the shower, and wrap myself in a towel. I hear my phone ringing in the other room, and I rush to answer it before voicemail picks it up.

"Hello?" I ask with a little confusion, because I don't recognize the number displayed on the screen.

"Kiara? It's Jenny."

"Hey, Jenny... is everything all right?" I ask.

"Yes, everything's fine. I just feel awful for the attitude I've been giving you lately. It has nothing to do with you. I just had so much going on lately... I was stressed, and I took it out on the wrong people. I'm so sorry."

"It's all right," I assure her. "I completely understand."

"Thank you, Kiara. Do you think we could get together sometime and talk? I could use a friend right now, and I don't know anyone else right now... I'm always so busy with work and school... I'm sure you understand that, too."

"Absolutely," I agree. "I'm always here if you need to talk. Do you want to meet at the restaurant early in the morning for coffee? Or we could go to the café for lunch again."

"Would you be able to meet me somewhere tonight?" she asks nervously. "I know it's short notice, but I could use someone to talk to."

*Shit.* "I'm so sorry, Jenny. I already made plans this evening... I'm meeting a friend from culinary school. We're going to practice pastries," I lie. "I'd invite you to join us, but I'm going to her house and I'm not sure how she'd feel about it."

"No, that's okay," Jenny replies quickly. "We can meet for lunch tomorrow."

I'm filled with guilt and quickly backtrack. "Jenny, if you need me, I can cancel."

"I'll be okay," she assures me. "Enjoy your time with your friend, and I'll see you tomorrow."

Robbs is sitting in front of his oversized flat-screen television watching Monday night football when his phone rings. "Did you talk to her?" he answers, after looking at the name on his screen.

"Yes, I just hung up with her," Jenny replies. "I also called the restaurant and asked to speak with Paul. Megan said he's taking the day off. Kiara gave me a lame story about having plans with a girl from her school. I'm almost positive they're meeting up tonight."

"So it's go time?" Robbs has been waiting for this moment since he first shot the video of Jenny and Paul together.

"It's go time," she agrees. "Did you find her address?"

"Yep. I saved the route to her apartment in my GPS. Are you sure you want to do this? Once I show her the video, I can't unshow it. I don't want you to regret it after and whine about how we went too far."

"I'm positive," Jenny assures him. "Take the bitch down a few pegs and I'll do nothing but celebrate."

"How about I call you after?" Robbs suggests. "You can bring your fine ass over here and we can celebrate together."

"You're on."

# Chapter Eight

I stand in front of my full-length mirror and examine myself. My new, dark denim skinny jeans make my ass appear plump and firm, and the emerald shirt showcases my 36C breasts perfectly. Since Paul only ever sees my hair up in a bun in the kitchen, I decided to wear it loose around my shoulders for our date.

It's *not* a date, I think, catching myself. It's just two people enjoying a meal together... just like last night, only a different setting. I fasten a silver bracelet around my left wrist and pull my new brown leather boots from their box. As I tug the left one on, my doorbell rings.

What the fuck? I check the time. It's only six o'clock. Paul and I aren't going out until seven-thirty, and the plan is for us to meet at the restaurant.

"Hold on," I call out as I pull the boot back off. I make my way to the door and peek through the peephole. Robbs is on the other side, tapping his foot impatiently. I fling the door open.

"What the hell are you doing here?" I demand.

"Now, now," Robbs chides me. He pushes his way past me and into the apartment. "Is that any way to welcome a guest?"

"The word 'guest' would imply that you'd been invited," I reply harshly. I shut the door behind me as I turn toward him. "I don't recall inviting you, so answer my fucking question. And while you're at it, you can explain how you found out where I live."

"You'd be surprised by what you can learn on the Internet," he answers sharply. "Kiara, I'm here as a friend. There's no need for all of this hostility."

"I have a hard time believing that. Since when the hell have we been friends?"

"I know I'm an ass at the restaurant, but you shouldn't take it personally," Robbs insists. "I do admire your talents in the kitchen, but you're the competition, and I've been treating you accordingly... you know, it's considered good manners to offer your guests something to drink."

"I'm not planning on you being around long enough to finish a drink, but there's some bottled water in the fridge. Help yourself if you want one."

Robbs walks into my kitchen and retrieves a cold bottle. "This is a quaint place you keep here," he comments as he returns to the living room. "Small... but charming." He opens the bottle and takes a drink.

"Cut to the chase, Robbs. Why are you here?" I ask impatiently.

"I'm here because I'm worried about you, Kiara. I see the way Paul looks at you at Fission. And a person would need to be blind and deaf to miss the way he flirts with you. Last night, I noticed you returning those looks. I think you should know what kind of guy you're dealing with."

"Paul may flirt with me, but it's harmless," I insist. "And even if it wasn't, it's none of your business."

"We're competing for a spot as Paul's apprentice, so I feel that it's very much my business," Robbs argues. "And I know things about our boss... things that would make you never want to set foot in the restaurant again, much less flirt with the asshole."

"I know that people at Fission gossip about him, Robbs. There's nothing you can tell me that I haven't already heard. But I don't put much stock in gossip... though I'm not surprised that you do."

"I've heard stories from Amy and Charlotte too, but that's not why I'm here. If you can look me in the eye and honestly say there's no part of you that's tempted to give in to Paul's advances, then I'll leave right now. But if there IS a part of you that's considering being with him... even a small part... then there's something I need to show you."

His last statement got my attention. "Show me...?" I ask slowly.

Robbs pulls his phone from his jeans' pocket. "Show you..."

What the hell. Let him play whatever game he wants and maybe he'll leave. "And what is this earth-shattering video you have for me?"

"I'm glad you ask," Robbs says, smiling sadly. "You're making the right decision. I know you stayed late at the restaurant with Paul last night. Jenny and I had a drink after we finished up, and I left my phone at our booth. I went back a few hours later and saw your car pull out of the parking lot when I drove up."

"We spent a long time cleaning," I explain quickly.

"I'm sure you did," he says, nodding. "That's not why I'm here, though it does make me wonder if I'm too late." He takes another long drink from the bottle and stares at me intently.

"Go on..."

"The front door was unlocked, so I let myself in and grabbed my phone. I hit the head, sat in there for a while and checked the messages I'd missed... logged in to Facebook... you know the drill. Anyway, when I was finished, I opened the bathroom door slowly. I didn't want Paul to know I was there. Frankly, I didn't feel like talking to the bastard. But to my surprise, I stepped into the dining room and found Paul and Jenny at the bar."

"Jenny?" I ask in shock. "What was she doing there?"

"Paul," Robbs answers simply.

My mouth drops in disbelief. This can't be happening. There's no way he slept with Jenny after our dinner last night. "I don't believe you," I tell Robbs.

"I don't imagine you would," he says with a nod, "but you can see if for yourself." He holds his phone out to me. "All you have to do is push play."

A part of me, a big part, doesn't want to see what is on his phone. If I don't see it, it's not real. But curiosity combined with my need to protect myself takes over, and I take the phone from Robbs' hand. I swipe the screen to reveal a still shot of Paul and Jenny at the bar. Paul stands behind it while Jenny perches on a stool.

"You may want to sit down," Robbs warns.

I take a seat on my sofa and push play. I watch Jenny and Paul speak, their hands entwined.

"Is there any audio?" I ask Robbs, desperate to hear the conversation.

He shakes his head and takes a seat beside me. "You won't want to hear it anyway," he assures me.

Jenny moves onto the top of the bar, followed quickly by Paul. My heart breaks as I watch them strip off their clothes and go at it like animals.

"Kiara?" Robbs says softly. "Do you want to turn it off now? I think you've seen enough."

I shake my head without taking my eyes off of the screen. I need to see everything, to know exactly what happened. We watch the rest of the video in silence until, finally, it ends. Robbs puts an arm around me and I'm too upset to shake him off.

"Kiara, I'm so sorry. I know the video is graphic, but I also knew that you had to see it."

"Do either of them know you filmed this?" I ask softly.

"No," he assures me. "After they finished, I ducked down in a booth and hid until Jenny left and Paul went back to the kitchen. Then I snuck out the front door."

"*Why* did you film them?"

"Because what Paul is doing is wrong. I think he needs to be stopped. I knew if I didn't have concrete proof, people would assume that I was accusing him of things because I'm not doing well in the completion. Though I think what I have here proves that I'm not doing well because I don't, shall we say, have the right equipment."

"Thank you for showing this to me, Robbs," I say as I rise to my feet. "If you'll excuse me, I have some phone calls to make."

Jenny paces the floors of her small apartment, waiting for the phone to ring. When it finally does, she answers it quickly. "Is it done?"

"It's done," Robbs informs her. "I think we've seen the last of Kiara. Now get your ass over here so we can celebrate."

<<◇>>

I wake to the sound of my phone ringing. I roll over, see Paul's number on the screen, and silence the call. I check the time on my bedside alarm clock. It's seven-thirty in the morning. I yawn, stretch, and try to hold back my tears as the memories of that video fill my head.

After Robbs left last night, I spent a long time trying to figure out what to do. I wasn't ready to face Paul, so I stood him up and ignored his calls. I know I have to face him, so I retrieve my phone and listen to his messages.

"Kiara, it's a quarter to eight. I'm just wondering where you're at. I've got us a table, call me if you're lost and I'll give you directions. See you soon."

"Kiara, it's eight now, and I'm really starting to worry about you. Please call me back as soon as you get this message."

The next voicemail came through at nine o'clock. "Kiara, I'm incredibly worried about you. If you don't call me back soon, I'm going to start calling the hospitals and police stations."

I'm oddly satisfied to hear the worry in his voice. Let the bastard suffer for a while. I start the fourth message.

"Kiara, I don't know what's going on. I know that you're not at any of the hospitals, but I'm still afraid that something's happened to you. Please, please call me as soon as possible. If you've decided you don't want to spend time with me, that's all right. I'll understand. I just need to know that you're all right."

"You're just worried that I've caught on to your slime ball ways," I scream into my receiver to no one. I click on the message he left a few minutes ago.

"Kiara, this is Paul again. I finally got a hold of Jenny last night, and she said you had plans with a friend from culinary school. Was I confused about our plans? I thought we were meeting for dinner last night, but if I was mistaken, I'm sorry for all of the messages. Call me back, or I'll just see you when you come in to work today."

I can tell by the tone of his voice that he knows damn well he wasn't confused about our plans. He knows I stood him up on purpose, and he's panicked. My phone rings again, and once again I silence it. I know I have to face him, but I want to do it face-to-face. I want him to look me in the eye and admit to what he did.

I roll out of bed and carefully select my clothes for the day. I pull on my new skinny jeans and a tight cowl-necked sweater that accentuates my curves. It's not an outfit I'd work in, but I'm not planning on doing any cooking today.

I ride the elevator downstairs, climb in my car, and drive toward Fission. On my way, I call Chef Lee's office.

"Hello?" she answers on the second ring.

"Good morning, Chef Lee. This is Kiara Sands."

"Hello, Kiara! It's so good to hear from you. I've been wondering how things are going at Fission. Your weekly reports from Chef Weston have been phenomenal. I'm so proud of you! Are you enjoying the experience?"

"That's actually why I'm calling, Chef Lee," I tell her. "I was hoping you have room in your schedule to meet with me this afternoon. There are some things I'd like to discuss."

"Let me check..." After a long pause, she returns to the line. "I can meet with you at three-thirty. Will that work with your schedule at the restaurant?"

"That will be perfect, thank you," I answer.

"Great, I'll see you then."

I disconnect the call just as I pull into the parking lot of Fission. It's eight-thirty, and Paul's car is the only one in the lot. I'm thankful no one else is here. I have a lot to say and I don't want to be overheard by Amy, Charlotte, or any of the other nosey, gossiping staff.

I push the front door, and I'm relieved to find it is unlocked. The dining room is dark and quiet. Any other time, I'd find the atmosphere peaceful, but this morning it just seems sad and lonely. I walk into the kitchen and find Paul sitting on a stool next to the prep station. He looks up as the door swings shut behind me.

"Kiara, thank God," he says as he rushes toward me. "I've been so worried. I didn't sleep at all last night." He wraps his arms around me.

"Don't fucking touch me," I tell him as I escape from his embrace.

"Kiara, what's wrong?" Confusion fills his face. "Has something happened? Were you in an accident? I called over and over again. Have you lost your phone?"

"You know exactly what happened," I answer hatefully, "and now, so do I."

"What are you talking about? I don't know anything. Did I do something to upset you? Is that why you didn't show last night? If I overstepped, if you feel like us hanging out together is inappropriate, I understand."

"What's inappropriate is that you fucked Jenny on the bar Sunday night," I say firmly.

All of the color drains from his face. "Kiara, I didn't..."

"Save it, there's no point in lying. I didn't come here to listen to your excuses. I just wanted to bring this back," I tell him as I pull my folded Fission chef's jacket from my bag. "I have no interest in being yet another employee you screw and then screw over. Consider this my resignation," I say as I throw the jacket at his face.

He catches it and lays it across the prep table. "Kiara, I don't know what Jenny told you, but it didn't happen the way you think it did. I admit I slept with her. And it was wrong. That was one of the incidents I was talking about when I told you I've made mistakes."

"No, it wasn't," I argue. "You fucked her after I left Sunday. I know you did. What happened, Paul? I didn't drop my pants fast enough for you, so you moved on to Jenny? Did you at least wait until I left the parking lot before you called her, or had you already made plans with her before we had dinner together?"

"That night with Jenny was weeks ago," Paul insists. "It was before I thought I had a chance with you... she asked me to help her study for her pairings class, and we got way too drunk. Things went too far, but it didn't mean anything. You're the one I care about, Kiara."

"I see," I reply angrily. "So Jenny was just a fuck for you. That speaks volumes about your character, Paul."

"I understand if you don't want to spend time with me outside of the restaurant," he says with a sigh, "but please don't quit the program. You deserve to be here, Kiara. And working here would be a big boost for your career. Please don't throw away this opportunity because I made a mistake."

"The winner of this competition will be your new apprentice, and I'd rather light my hair on fire than work for you," I hiss. "I've scheduled a meeting with my faculty adviser at *Cordon Bleu*. Hopefully, I can make up the last month of classes and finish out the rest of this semester. If not, I'll take an incomplete and start over in January. Regardless, I won't be setting foot in this place again."

I turn around, slam the swinging doors open, and step back into the dining room. I glance at the bar and feel like I'm going to be sick.

"Kiara."

I turn and see Paul in the doorway. "Don't follow me," I demand. I rush out of the restaurant and nearly run Jenny over on the sidewalk.

"Good morning..." she greets me awkwardly. "Are you leaving?"

"Yes," I hiss as I walk past her and step into the parking lot.

"Is everything all right? When are you coming back?"

I turn on her. "Everything is fucking perfect, especially for you. After all of that talk in the café about how we shouldn't screw our way to the top, you turn around and do exactly that."

"Look, Kiara... I can explain," she insists.

"I don't need to hear your pathetic explanations. I know exactly what happened. Your 'I'm not sure this is what I want' bullshit was just a line to get me to let my guard down. You're jealous of my cooking skills, and you're jealous Paul found me more attractive than you. You knew that the only way you had a chance in hell of winning the apprenticeship was if you screwed the boss. So you win, Jenny. You can have the job and you can have Paul. You deserve each other, and I deserve better." I turn and walk toward my car.

"Kiara, wait..." she calls out.

I leave the parking lot without looking back.

# Chapter Nine

"Kiara, this is quite surprising," Chef Lee says with obvious disappointment. "Out of all of my students, I thought you'd be best suited for this competition. Do you realize how many of your classmates wanted that spot at Fission?"

"I understand, Chef Lee. And I'm sorry," I apologize, "but the environment at Fission is not one I can work in. There's a lot of... internal politics at play."

"Is the environment hostile?" Chef Lee asks. "Should I contact the labor board?"

I shake my head. "There's no need to do that. Nothing going on there is illegal... exactly."

"Kiara, I'd love to help you out, but first you're going to have to tell me the full story. You're obligated to Fission for the next eight weeks, and your semester grade depends on you completing the competition. I may be able to pull some strings, but only if I know the facts of the situation."

"Chef Weston seems more interested in how his female candidates perform outside of the kitchen," I say firmly.

"I see," says Chef Lee, perplexed. "And I assume you're not talking about the front of the house?"

I shake my head. "If I can't make up my work here this semester, I understand. I'll start over in January. But I can't go back to that restaurant."

"Kiara, I don't mean to pry into your personal business, but did you develop a physical relationship with Chef Weston?"

"No, I did *not*."

"But you felt pressured to do so in order to win the apprenticeship?"

"I felt that the events occurring outside of the competition were detrimental to my success. Chef Weston showed obvious favoritism to me, and he made it clear that he was interested in me in a nonprofessional way. That favoritism and interest caused the other competitors to develop hostile attitudes toward me. I can't prove it, but I'm certain my work was sabotaged at least once."

"At some point, you're going to have to learn to work in hostile environments," Chef Lee advises. "Professional kitchens are notorious for drama. I'd have thought you already knew that."

"I understand," I assure her. "But Chef Weston's actions have made me completely uninterested in being his apprentice. I feel that continuing in the competition would be a waste of my time."

Chef Lee stares at me intently and is silent for quite some time. "Very well. I'll need you to write an official statement detailing why you are leaving the competition. You don't have to get specific with the details of Chef Weston's flirtations, but I'll need something for your file."

"I can do that," I agree.

"I must warn you, Kiara, you're going to face some scrutiny from your classmates. You've missed four weeks of class, and most people in that situation would have to take an incomplete for the semester. I'm willing to let you make up the work you've missed, but I can't give you any other special treatment. Midterms are next week… you'll have to have all of your make-up work turned in before then, and you have to take the tests as scheduled."

"Thank you, Chef Lee," I say with relief. "I understand. I'll get started right away, and I'll be prepared for the exams."

"I certainly hope so, Kiara. You're incredibly talented, and I'd hate to see this set your graduation date back. I will email you a list of make-up assignments. You can do the written work online, providing you log in to the system with your webcam on so no one can accuse you of cheating. The practical assignments can be made up during my planning periods."

"Thank you, Chef Lee. I know this is a huge inconvenience to you."

"Wait until after next week's exams to thank me," Chef Lee answers impatiently. "You're incredibly talented, but I confess I'll be surprised if you're able to complete all of your work on time and prepare for your midterms. As your advisor, I must reemphasize that the best thing you could do is set aside your personal issues and complete your time at Fission."

"I understand but I just can't," I tell her again. "I will get all of my work finished on schedule. And as for my exams, it's not like I've taken four weeks off from cooking. I'll surprise you, I promise."

"We'll see, Kiara. We'll see."

"Time's up, pencils down," Chef Lee announces from the front of the classroom. Over the last two hours, my classmates and I have been taking our midterm practical test. I have to admit I wasn't as prepared as I thought I'd be.

"Please step away from your desks and move to your work station," Chef Lee continues. We stand and do as she directed. I arrive at my work station and find an assortment of ingredients spread out on the table.

"This is a three-hour practical exam," Chef Lee explains, "during which time you will complete a variety of dishes that comprise a full-course meal. The salad course will showcase your knife skills, and all dressings must be made from scratch. Following that, you will create all five of the mother sauces. You will reserve a sample of each before taking two sauces of your choosing and turning them into small sauces. Those sauces are to be served with a dish of your choosing, both of which must have meat components. Finally, you will create an ice cream, sorbet, or gelato. Once you've moved on to the next stage of the exam, you may not go back and correct any of the other stages. Your time starts now."

I survey the ingredients that are already at my station. Everything needed for the mother sauces is already there. I set pans to warm on my stovetop before rushing to the walk-in for my salad ingredients. I want to make a classic Caesar, so I grab romaine, parmesan, lemons, mustard, and Worcestershire sauce. I stop in the pantry for anchovies before returning to my station.

I finish the salad quickly and begin on my sauces. While I work, I consider which sauces I want to use in my next course. I know most of my classmates will be tempted to create a simple cream sauce, as it's the least time consuming. I want my work to stand out, so I decide my entrée dishes will include beef with a *Bordelaise* sauce, which will be created from my *Espagnole*, and poached salmon with a *Maltaise* sauce, which I will make from my *Hollandaise*.

I complete the mother sauces and reserve samples of them as Chef Lee had instructed. I return to the walk-in for beef tenderloin, mushrooms, salmon, and asparagus. I return to my workstation and my heart sinks. My reserved *Veloute* sauce has broken in its bowl. There's nothing I can do about it now, I just have to move on and make sure everything else is perfect.

I glance up at the front of the classroom and see Chef Lee grading the written exams at her desk. I'll know whether I've passed or failed before I leave for the evening. I wasn't as prepared as I should have been for the written portion of the midterm. That, combined with my broken *Veloute*, sends anxiety coursing through my body.

Just keep it together. It's all about the food. I know what I'm doing. I brown the tenderloin in a hot skillet and transfer it to the oven. The salmon will only need to cook for a few minutes. I prepare my poaching water, then return to the walk-in once more for my dessert ingredients. I enjoy savory tones in my final course, so I decide to prepare a pink grapefruit and sage sorbet. I gather the ingredients, return to my station, and check my tenderloin. I press it with a gloved finger and can tell it's overcooked.

*Damn it!* I pull it out of the oven and leave it to rest on my cutting board. I slam the pan down and draw the attention of several of my classmates. "Sorry," I say sheepishly. This isn't going well at all, and a big part of me wants to give up. But if I have a prayer of finishing the semester, I have to complete this midterm. It'll all be over after today. I'll be caught up with everything and start fresh next week. By finals, I'll be kicking everyone's asses again.

The entrée portion of the exam must be completed before I can start on my sorbet, so I slide the salmon into my poaching liquid and add the necessary ingredients to my sauces. While the sauces simmer, I slice the tenderloin. It's still pink in the middle, and I'm slightly encouraged. I let the asparagus steam while I plate my beef dish. Once I'm satisfied with my entrées, I set them aside and move on to my final course.

I make a simple syrup on the stovetop and juice the grapefruits into it. I toss in the sage and let the flavors meld for a few minutes. While the mixture simmers, I glance back at my bowls of mother sauces… everything but the *Veloute* is still intact.

I hear a noise at the front of the room and look up to see Chef Lee leaving her desk. "You have thirty minutes left. As you should all be on the dessert portion of the exam, I'm going to start sampling your other courses."

She walks up to my station and I'm relieved that she is tasting my entrées while they're still hot. I'm also relieved that I'm too busy with my sorbet to watch her reactions to my food. I strain the simple syrup mixture into a glass bowl and transfer it to the ice cream machine at my station. There's nothing left for me to do but wait.

Once again, I wake to the sound of my chiming phone. I've had a restless night, and the noise startles me.

"Hello?"

"Kiara, this is Arabella Lee. I'd like for you to come in to discuss your midterm grade."

"Yes, Chef, of course. Is there a problem?"

"I'd rather discuss it in person, Kiara. Can you be here in an hour? If not, I can meet you at four o'clock, after my advanced pastry class."

"I can be there in an hour," I assure her.

"Thank you, I'll see you then."

The line goes dead, and my heart fills with panic. I know I didn't do well on the written exam, but I'd felt confident about the practical. I jump out of bed and pull on the first set of clothes I find in my unfolded pile of laundry… baggy jeans and a soft, frumpy sweatshirt. I slide my feet into my laceless Converse and examine myself in the mirror. My face is pale, and I have dark circles under my eyes. I dab on some concealer and lip gloss and make my way to the kitchen.

I have no appetite, so I pour myself a glass of orange juice and start a pot of coffee. It will only take me fifteen minutes to drive to the college. I spend twenty minutes pacing the floor and going over the practical exam in my head. I'd tasted all of my dishes, so I know my flavors were well developed. My sorbet was slightly grainy, but it had been delicious all the same.

I glance at my phone and see that it is twenty-five minutes till nine. I pour coffee into a travel mug and head out the door. The drive to the college is uneventful, and I arrive at Chef Lee's office five minutes before our scheduled time. I knock lightly on the door.

"Come in," she calls out.

I open the door and find her sitting behind her desk. She's on the phone, so I wave my greeting.

"Thank you," she says to the person on the other line. "I'll speak with her and get back with you."

"Good morning, Kiara," she greets me as she returns the phone to its cradle. "Thank you for coming in on such short notice."

"Of course, Chef Lee... you said you need to speak with me about my midterm?"

"Yes," she replies, studying me carefully. "How do you feel you did?"

"I know I could have done better on my written exam... and I know my *Veloute* sauce broke. Other than that, I feel like I did all right," I answer.

"And is 'all right' acceptable to you?"

"No," I admit meekly.

"Kiara, you know I have a soft spot for you. But your exam results were quite disappointing."

"I understand," I reply, lowering my head.

"You passed the midterm, but just barely. Your current course grades are so low that it will be next to impossible for you to receive anything but B's and C's on your finals. And while you'll be able to continue on next semester..."

"I'm going to lose my scholarships," I finish the sentence for her.

"Yes, I'm afraid there's only one sure-fire way that you'll be able to retain your financial aid package," she tells me.

"What's that?" I ask quickly. "I'm willing to do whatever it takes, Chef Lee. You've been so understanding about the situation at Fission. I'll do anything you ask."

"I was on the phone with Chef Weston when you arrived," she begins and my heart sinks. I know where this conversation is going. "He takes full responsibility for the actions that led you to leave his competition. He's willing to let you return to Fission. You've only missed six days of work there, which you could easily make up. Is that something you're willing to consider?"

"I don't know..." I hesitate. "May I have some time to think about it?"

"You may have a day or two," Chef Lee agrees. "I understand this isn't what you want, but I'm afraid you may have no other choice... unless, of course, you apply for student loans to pay for the remainder of your education. You need to decide if avoiding the restaurant is worth tens of thousands of dollars to you."

I let out a long sigh. Hearing it put that way makes me see my situation in a new light, but I still can't bear the thought of working in a kitchen with Paul and Jenny. "I'll have my answer to you by tomorrow."

"Take until Monday, if you need to," Chef Lee offers. "If you come to a decision before then, call me on my cell."

"Thank you, Chef Lee," I say as I rise from my seat. "I know I've been a difficult student this semester."

"I just want to see you succeed, Kiara," she says kindly. "Please consider your options carefully."

# Chapter Ten

I sit at my desk and stare blankly at the screen of my laptop. It's Saturday night, and I've been researching student loans since I left Chef Lee's office the previous morning. The information I've found is discouraging, but I still can't imagine walking back in to Fission. I feel a pang in my stomach and realize I haven't eaten today, so I walk in to the kitchen and survey the contents of my refrigerator. I decide on scrambled eggs, which I make quickly and eat directly from the skillet. I finish and toss the skillet into my sink as my doorbell chimes.

Who the hell could that be? I remember the last time I had an unexpected visitor. I walk to the door and say a silent prayer that Robbs isn't waiting on the other side again. I look through the peephole and see Jenny. That's even worse.

I decide to pretend I'm not home. I take a seat on my sofa and wait for her to leave.

"Kiara?" she calls out loudly. "I know you're home. Your car is in the parking lot and your neighbor says you haven't left all day. Please let me in. I'm not leaving until you listen to what I have to say."

I stomp over and swing the door open. "What do you want?"

"Can I come in?" Jenny asks with hesitation.

"I think you've already proven you'll do whatever the hell you want," I snap harshly as I move back to the sofa. She steps into the apartment and shuts the door behind her. She stares at me intently before speaking again.

"Are you all right, Kiara?" she asks. "You look awful."

I glance down at my clothes. I'm wearing plaid flannel pajama pants and the same sweatshirt I wore to my meeting with Chef Lee. I know my hair is a mess, and I can't imagine the circles under my eyes have improved since I last checked in the mirror.

"Thank you for the critique of my appearance," I say with a sneer. "If that's all you came for, you can leave now."

"Kiara, don't be ridiculous. I'm sorry. I'm just worried about you."

"I'm sure you are," I reply sarcastically. "You're such a selfless, charitable person. If you're here to check on me, you needn't have bothered, I'm just fine."

"I know you're pissed at me, and you have every right to be," Jenny says softly. "And I know you're in trouble at school. I overheard Paul talking to your instructor yesterday."

"Ah... tell me, were you under Paul when you overheard him? Or do the two of you save that for after hours?"

"I deserved that," Jenny replies anxiously. "But nothing's going on between Paul and me. I came here to explain that video you saw."

"So you know Robbs caught the two of you."

"Kiara... I knew Robbs was filming us that night. I *meant* for Robbs to film us."

"*What?*"

Tears fill Jenny's eyes. "This is the worst thing I've ever done. It was all Robbs' idea. We were both so jealous of the way Paul treated you, and we thought you'd win the apprenticeship. Robbs convinced me that we had to stop you, that we had to find a way to make you quit."

"Let me get this straight," I interrupt her. "You were afraid I'd sleep with Paul and win the apprenticeship because of it. You resented that idea, so you decided the best way to deal with it was sleeping with him first?"

"I know... looking back now, I can see it was hypocritical and devious. I can't apologize enough for what I did. But it's no reason to sacrifice your education. Come back to the restaurant... please?"

I shake my head. "I don't care what your motivations were. Paul still slept with you. He wined and dined me after work, and then had sex with you as soon as I left.”

“That's not what happened, Kiara. That's what I came to tell you.”

“I saw the video, Jenny.”

“I know, but Robbs lied about *when* it happened. Paul and I had sex way before you started showing interest in him.”

The pieces all fall into place in my head, and I begin to understand. “It happened right before he started acting so distant toward you,” I say softly.

Jenny nods. “And it was all me, Kiara. I seduced him. I asked him to help me study for a pairings class because I knew the only way I had a chance with him was if he was drunk. I kept the evening going, kept asking for more samples and bigger shots of vodka. And even after all of the booze, I still had to talk him into having sex with me. That's why there's no audio on the video Robbs showed you. We didn't want you to hear me convincing him that it was okay.”

“So everything Paul said when I confronted him was true?”

Jenny nods. “It's been awful at Fission since you left. Paul is devastated. He sulks around the kitchen and snaps at everyone who tries to talk to him. And we didn't even have a cooking competition this week. He said his heart just wasn't in it. Please, come back.”

I sit silently for a moment, absorbing what I've just learned. "Jenny, I'm glad you came over to explain this. But there are parts that I'm still not understanding. Like why in the world you'd ever join forces with Robbs."

"He got me riled up over the fact that Paul was showing you so much favoritism. At first, I thought he was crazy. But he got me to agree to help him, if he could prove that Paul was unfairly favoring you... that day you were covering the prep station..."

"He's the one who pulled the cutting board over the edge of the table. He's the reason all of the food fell to the floor. He blatantly sabotaged me, and you were okay with that?"

"I was being selfish." She's sobbing again, and I feel that she's truly sorry for what she did. "I wasn't thinking about the situation being unfair to you. When Paul hugged you after the food fell, then made ME help fix the mistake, I was convinced that Robbs was right... that you'd win the apprenticeship regardless of how well he and I cooked."

"I should have known Robbs was up to something when he showed up here with that video. I came so close to not watching it... I didn't trust him. But he gave me a long speech about his attitude at Fission not being personal, and claimed that he was trying to protect me. I should never have let him through the door."

"He would have made sure you saw the video no matter what," Jenny says gravely. "I'm so sorry... I know I keep saying that, but I want you to understand. Robbs has been even more smug and hateful since you quit. If for no other reason, you should come back to work to kick his ass in the competition."

"How much of this does Paul know?"

"None of it," she admits. "He hasn't asked me how you found out that we slept together. And to his credit, he hasn't taken out any of his frustrations on me specifically. If he did, I'd deserve it. I think he might actually be in love with you, Kiara. If you were ever interested in him at all, you should go talk to him... he's probably still at Fission."

I stand and grab my purse.

"Does this mean that you're coming back to work?" Jenny asks hopefully.

"I don't know. But you're right. I need to talk to him."

I speed all the way to Fission and arrive in record time. With the exception of Paul's black Land Rover, the parking lot is empty. I pull into a spot, jump out of my car, and rush to the front door. As usual, it's unlocked. I let myself in, run through the dining room, and barrel through the kitchen doors. Paul is bent over the sink, scrubbing a saucepan. I clear my throat and he jumps before turning around.

"Kiara?" he asks in surprise. "What are you doing here?"

"Oh, Paul," I cry and throw myself into his arms. "I had to come talk to you. I'm so sorry!"

He holds me tightly and caresses the back of my head. "What's the matter, Kiara?" he asks in a soothing voice. "Is it your midterm? I spoke with Chef Lee yesterday. I told her that you're welcome to come back to work here."

"It's not the midterm," I answer with a sob. "It's everything else. I talked to Jenny. I know I was wrong about when the two of you hooked up. I know you weren't lying when I confronted you that day."

"Thank god," Paul says, holding me even tighter. "I'm so sorry, Kiara, I never should have been with her. It's you who I've wanted all along. I've been infatuated with you since the moment I saw you sitting at the back table. Your incredible talent in the kitchen just made me want you more. Will you ever be able to forgive me?"

I pull away slightly and look into his clear blue eyes. "I already have."

His eyes light up and a broad smile spreads across his face. He leans down and kisses me softly… his lips on mine feel better than anything I've ever imagined. I open my lips slightly and tease his tongue with mine. Shivers coarse through my body, and I feel as if I'm going to collapse in his arms. I slip my hands down to his chef's jacket… my fingers fumble as I try to undo the first button and he pulls away suddenly.

"We can't do this, not like this," he whispers, still holding me.

"I know," I say, agreeing with a disappointed nod. "If I'm going to rejoin the competition, we can't get involved."

Paul lets out a laugh. "That's not what I'm talking about. Come sit down with me," he says, pulling me toward the group of stools arranged around the prep table. We each take a seat and he continues.

"I'll figure out how to go forward impartially with the competition. That's not why I just stopped you from undressing me," he explains with a sly grin. "I stopped you because I want to do this right. I know you've been through a lot in your life. I know you're hesitant to trust people. And you know I've made more than my share of mistakes with women in the past. I think we should take things slowly. I want to prove myself worthy of you. When we finally make love, I don't want there to be a doubt in your mind about my feelings for you. Does that sound like something you'd be interested in?"

With tears in my eyes, I nod and fall back into his arms.

# Chapter Eleven

Jenny and I sit at our usual back table and drink coffee before our shifts start. It's Thursday, my fourth day back at Fission.

"Are you ready for today's challenge?" I ask her.

"I hope so," she replies with a nod. "But as usual, as long as one of us kicks Robbs' ass, I'll be satisfied."

I've been able to forgive Jenny for the part she played in all of the drama, but I'm still having a hard time being civil to Robbs. Every time I see him, I remember the smug look of satisfaction he had on his face after he showed me the video. I still haven't told Paul that his night with Jenny was a set up, and I don't intend to. I also haven't shared with him that Robbs sabotaged my prep work that day. I know it would be an easy way to get Robbs kicked out of the competition, but it will be more satisfying to kick his ass and win the apprenticeship.

"How are things going with Paul?" Jenny asks.

"Perfect," I say. "We still haven't consummated our relationship, and I have to admit that I'm enjoying all of the courting. He opens doors for me, pulls my chair out at tables... I feel like I'm living in a romantic, Victorian-era movie."

"I've never had a man treat me like that," Jenny says.

"You will," I assure her. "You just have to stop discounting yourself. Demand to be treated with respect, and you will be."

Jenny and I have gotten closer over the last week, but I still haven't worked up the courage to ask her the question that's been nagging me. The way Robbs looks at her leads me to believe there was more to their relationship than planning my downfall, but I don't want to bring up a sore subject with her. If anything physical did happen between them, I'm sure it's over now.

"You may have to remind me of that next time I start dating someone," she says.

"I will." I smile. "That's what friends are for."

We each take a long drink of our coffees, and Robbs walks through the front door.

"The asshole has arrived," I tell Jenny. She turns and we watch Robbs pour a cup of coffee behind the bar and take a seat at his own table. His shit talking has stopped completely since I returned. He still sneers at me every chance he gets, but his silence has been a welcome change.

"You know, I heard him talking to Amy yesterday," Jenny tells me. "He called his faculty advisor and reported Paul's relationship with you. He insisted that it gives you an unfair advantage in the competition and asked if there was any legal action that could be taken. His instructor told him to grow a pair and stop complaining."

"That just makes me want to kick his ass even more. He's such a whiny little bitch," I observe. "Paul knew he'd try to pull something like that. He's been trying to come up with a way to make the competition fair."

"After what Robbs and I did to you, it would be fair for us both to be thrown out on our asses," Jenny says.

"Jenny, I told you I forgive you for that. There's no reason for you to keep bringing it up," I remind her.

"You're a better friend than I deserve, Kiara," she says.

"Don't worry. I'm sure I'll fuck up eventually and then you can have a chance to forgive me." I laugh.

Paul walks out of the kitchen and joins us at the table. "Good morning, ladies. Are you ready for today's cooking challenge?"

"We hope so," I reply. I want to kiss him hello so badly, but we agreed to maintain professional behavior when we're at work. I am positive everyone at the restaurant knows that we're seeing each other, but neither of us wants to fuel the gossip flames.

"Robbs, get over here. We're about to get started," Paul calls across the room.

Robbs slinks over. "I don't know why we're even bothering with this anymore. We all know that you're going to choose your girlfriend's dish."

Instead of returning Robbs' snarky attitude, Paul smiles. "I thought you might feel that way, so I won't be judging the competitions anymore. I'll be tasting your plates, of course, but Patrick and Claire will choose the winning dish."

"That's more than fair," Jenny assures him.

Paul turns to Robbs. "You would do well to remember that your attitude will be a factor in the final decision of who will win the apprenticeship."

"Yes, Chef," he answers half-heartedly.

"Excellent," says Paul, smiling. "Now, as I'm sure you realized when I mentioned Claire, we're having a dessert challenge today. I don't care what you make, as long as we don't already have a similar dish on the menu. You will have a full hour, and you must plate six portions. Your time starts now."

Jenny, Robbs, and I jump up and race to the kitchen. I've been expecting a dessert challenge, and I know exactly what I want to make. I race past my cooking station and go straight to the walk-in cooler. I grab eggs, cream, and butter before moving on to the pantry. There I get vanilla beans, flour, baking powder, and lavender buds.

I take my ingredients to my station and set them on the table. I set the oven to preheat, grease six small loaf pans, and shake flour into them. I mix my batter and finish just as the oven beeps to alert me that it's reached my desired temperature. I pour equal amounts of batter into each pan and place them on the top rack of the oven.

I glance at the clock and see that I still have forty minutes left. The cakes need to bake for twenty, and I need to come up with something to serve with them. I go back to the walk-in and survey the contents. I see a bag of Meyer lemons and decide that a frozen custard would be the perfect accompaniment to the cakes. I take three pieces of the fruit back to my station.

I glance in Jenny's direction and see that she seems confident. I can't tell what she's making, but two cartons of eggs sit at her station. I don't care what's going on at Robbs' station, so I don't bother looking his way.

Claire and Patrick are walking around the kitchen, while Paul sits quietly at the prep table. I start my custard base on the stovetop then grate the lemon zest into it. Meyer lemons are sweeter than regular lemons, so I decide to add a little of the juice as well. I let the ingredients simmer just long enough for the sugar to melt. I transfer the mixture to a shallow metal pan and then slide it in to the blast chiller.

I return to my station just as my timer beeps. I slip on two mitts and remove my desserts from the oven. I set them on a cooling rack and go back to the storage shelf for plates. I decide that the small, square plates will be a striking contrast to my round cakes and I take six of them back to my station. I gently turn the cakes out onto the plates and check the time. We have ten minutes left in the challenge, and I have nothing to do.

"There's a lot of waiting around involved with dessert making." Claire says as she approaches my station.

"Yes, Chef," I agree.

Claire moves closer to me and drops her voice. "I'm glad you came back, Kiara. And I want you to know that Paul is a good guy. Don't believe everything you hear around here. Charlotte's cousin applied for the pastry chef position at the same time I did. I know she has the wait-staff convinced that I slept my way into the job, but that couldn't be further from the case. My girlfriend and I have been together for six years," she adds.

"Thank you for telling me," I reply kindly. "And I've learned my lesson about listening to Amy and Charlotte." I wink.

"Good girl. You're going to go far in this field."

Claire moves on to Jenny's station and I once again check the time… we have five minutes left. I walk to the blast chiller, hoping my custard has had time to solidify. The cakes could be served on their own, but I think the addition of the custard will guarantee my win. I retrieve the pan and stop for an ice cream scoop on my way back to my station. I create six perfect spheres of custard, but leave them in the pan. I want to wait until the last possible second to plate them… the last thing I want is for them to melt and make my cakes soggy.

I look in Jenny's direction again. She has six perfect flans plated. I give in to temptation and glance at Robbs' station. He seems flustered, and the plates on his table are empty. He's bent over a large pan, cutting his cake into squares.

"You have sixty seconds," Patrick announces.

I count to thirty and place the custard on my plates.

"Time's up," Claire calls out. "Step away from your stations and move to the dining room."

We all obey and take seats at a round six top. Paul, Claire, and Patrick follow us, each carrying two plates.

"All right, Chefs, explain your dishes," Claire calls out.

Jenny goes first. "Today, I've prepared a maple-infused flan with a bourbon blueberry sauce."

Robbs clears his throat. "My dish is a maraschino chocolate cake, with just a hint of cayenne to keep things interesting."

"I made lavender-vanilla lava cakes with frozen Meyer-lemon custard," I say.

"These all look spectacular," Patrick compliments us. "Let's sample Kiara's dish before the custard melts."

I cut into my cake… the outside feels spongy and the filling oozes over my spoon. I add a touch of the custard and then sample my dish… it's as delicious as

I'd hoped it would be. And unlike my failed midterm sorbet, my custard is perfectly creamy.

"This is amazing," Claire says, her mouth still full of cake. The others nod in agreement.

We sample Jenny's flan next, and the moment I taste it, I know I have some serious competition.

"Have you ladies been practicing your desserts?" Patrick asks.

"We practice everything," Jenny answers confidently.

We move on to Robbs' cake. It's dry, and the 'touch' of cayenne sets my mouth on fire. The other chefs reach for their water glasses, and I know that Robbs' dish is definitely in third place.

"This is certainly interesting, Robbs," Claire says as her eyes water. "But I'm afraid you were a little heavy handed with the pepper. I suggest that in the future, you sample your batters before baking."

"Yes, Chef." Robbs' face is red, but I don't know if it's because of the heat of his cake or the embarrassment he feels at Claire's critique.

"If you'll excuse us, we're going to step into the kitchen and decide on a winner," Patrick announces. He and Claire rise from the table while Paul remains behind with us.

"Paul, I'd have no problem if you want to weigh in on their decision," Jenny tells him.

"That's quite all right," Paul says. "I'd hate for anyone to be accused of receiving favoritism. Besides, I trust Patrick and Claire completely... and I don't envy the position you and Kiara have put them in. This is the closest challenge we've had yet."

"Thank you," says Jenny, smiling.

Patrick and Claire return from the kitchen. "Before we announce the winner, I want both of you ladies to know that your dishes were divine," Claire begins. "In fact, I'd like to suggest to Paul that we put both of them on the permanent menu. It's time to change things up a bit, and I'm tired of cooking the same damn stuff all of the time."

"Thank you so much!" Jenny gushes.

"Thank you," Claire says. "Since both dishes were flawless, we based our decision on who successfully executed the most components. This week's winner is Kiara."

Paul smiles brightly at her announcement.

"Thank you so much," I say, beaming. I open my mouth to say more, but Robbs cuts me off.

"Now that the winner has been announced, could I please have my assignment for the day?" he asks Paul. "Or would you like me to go back to the kitchen and prove that I can make a chocolate cake?" he adds sarcastically.

"You know what? I'm in a generous mood today, Robbs," Paul answers. "I'm going to let all three of you decide who you'd like to work with today and throughout the weekend. I'll even let you choose first, Robbs, if the ladies don't have a problem with that."

"It's no problem for me," I reply.

"Me neither," Jenny agrees. "I'd be happy to work with anyone in the kitchen... well, almost anyone." She looks at Robbs.

"I'll work with Harrison then," Robbs says sharply. He pushes his chair away from the table and stomps into the kitchen.

"I'd like to work with Michael, if that's all right with you, Kiara," Jenny says. I suspect that Jenny has a bit of a crush on the Roast Chef, and I tell her that if she wants to work with him it's just fine with me.

"Michael won't be in for another half hour at least," Paul informs her, "which will give you plenty of time to share your flan recipe with Claire... I agree that both of your desserts should be put on our permanent menu."

"Thank you, Paul." Jenny says and turns to me. "Who are you going to work with this weekend? When you're not helping Claire with your dessert, that is?"

"I'm going to work with Cole," I announce. "It's time for me to learn how to make a sauce that won't break," I add.

I smile at Paul before Jenny and I set off for the kitchen to share our dessert recipes with Claire.

<<<>>>

"That was some impressive work you did at the restaurant today," Paul tells me. We're sitting on his comfortable, overstuffed leather sofa watching Top Chef. Paul loves culinary reality television as much as I do. It's just one of many things we have in common.

"Thank you, baby," I say.

His doorbell rings, and he jumps up from the couch. "That must be our Chinese food," he says as he crosses the room. We'd both had a long day at work, and we agreed that delivery was our best option for dinner. We haven't discussed whether or not I'm going to spend the night at his place, but it's getting late and I'm hoping that tonight will be 'our night' together.

Paul opens the door, hands the delivery man two twenties, and takes the bags from his hands.

"Oh my god, that smells delicious," I say as Paul deposits the bags on his coffee table. "What goes best with Chinese food, red wine or white?"

"White goes best with what I ordered for us," Paul explains. "But if you're going to drink, then I'm going to insist that you spend the night. I can crash on the couch, if that will make you more comfortable."

"We're both adults," I answer. "I think we can handle sleeping next to each other in the bed."

"I'm not so sure about that," he replies. He walks into his kitchen and retrieves plates, utensils, wine glasses, and a chilled bottle of chardonnay. He sets everything down on the table and returns to his seat next to me while I unpack the food.

"I'm so glad you came back to the restaurant," he tells me as he pours the wine. "We're going to have so much fun working together. And I'll be so glad when I can get rid of Robbs."

I laugh. "Be careful, the way you're talking, someone might think you've already chosen your new apprentice."

"But I'm not making the decisions anymore," he reminds me.

"Then how are you so sure I'm going to win?" I ask.

"Because you're the best," he replies.

I lean in to kiss him but his phone rings and interrupts us.

"God, I hope it's not someone at the restaurant." His frown turns to a smile when he checks his phone. "Hi, Mom," he answers happily.

I feel awkward listening in on his conversation, so I stand. "Bathroom," I whisper. He nods, and I make my escape. I don't actually need to use the restroom, so I check my makeup in the vanity mirror. The dark circles under my eyes have disappeared, and the gauntness is gone from my face. It's amazing what being happy can do for my appearance.

I crack open the bathroom door and listen for Paul's voice. The apartment is silent, so I'm fairly certain he's finished his call. I step back into the living room and see that he's enjoying a crab pot-sticker.

"Is everything all right with your family?" I ask as I return to my seat. "It's awfully late for your mom to be calling."

"She knows I usually work late in the kitchen. She always calls around this time," Paul explains. "And yes, everything's fine. She wanted to know if we were going to be able to make it to Thanksgiving."

"We...?" I ask. "So she knows about us?"

"Of course she does. I tell my mother everything... she even knows about what an ass I was. She's the one who advised me to take things slow with you."

I'm glad that Paul is close to his mother, but I'm not sure that I'm comfortable with her knowing all of the intimate details of our lives. "So what did you tell her... about Thanksgiving? I assumed we'd be working over the holidays."

Paul shakes his head. "I close the restaurant down on Thanksgiving, Christmas, and Easter. I don't feel right asking my employees to be away from their families."

"You have such a kind heart, baby," I tell him as I twist lo mien onto my fork. The food is salty and satisfying, and I chase it with my entire glass of wine.

"Slow down, baby," Paul teases me. "Are you okay? You threw that wine back like something's bothering you."

"I'm just a little jealous, I guess," I admit. "Sometimes I wish my mom was around to give me advice."

"Have you ever thought about trying to find your parents?" Paul asks softly.

I shake my head. "They left me. If they want to see me again, they can find me. For all I know, they're dead."

"I'm sorry, baby. Let's change the subject. It looks like Charlie and Sarah are in the running to win this week's challenge," he says as he gestures to the television.

"I hate Sarah," I say. "I hope Charlie kicks her ass."

We finish our meal in silence while we watch the drama play out before us. As I'd hoped, Charlie wins the competition.

"I'd love to be on one of these shows one day," I confess. "Or maybe one of the networks could shoot a show at Fission!"

"Oh my god, that's the last thing I'd ever want to do," Paul groans. "Think about it, all of the cameramen would get in our way."

"But it would be good for business," I argue playfully.

"Business is just fine." He smiles at me and once again I feel as if I could melt into the chair.

"What are you smiling about?" he asks after several moments.

"You," I answer. "I'm so happy when we're together, Paul. I feel like I'm living in a fairy tale."

"This is no fairy tale," Paul insists. "Fairy tales end. And I don't intend to ever stop making you happy."

I fall into his arms and our lips meet. We kiss softly… I lay down on the couch, pulling Paul on top of me. He runs one hand through my hair while the other grips my ass. I wrap my legs around his waist and lift my pelvis to his… I can feel his growing erection against my hip. I thrust back and forth against it.

He pulls away from me slightly. "Kiara..." he says, "if you keep doing that, I'm not going to be able to control myself."

"What makes you think I want you to control yourself?" I ask in my most seductive voice. "I know you want to take things slowly," I say as I continue rocking my hip back and forth against his throbbing cock. "So we can go as slowly as you'd like."

Paul climbs off of me, stands, and lifts me into his arms. "What are you doing?" I squeal in delight.

"I told you I want to do this right," he explains with a grin. "So I'm taking you to the bedroom." He carries me into his room, and we collapse together onto the bed. I reach for the hem of my T-shirt, and he covers my hand with his.

"Let me," he insists. He lifts the shirt over my head and tosses it to the floor. I sit up, and he reaches behind me and unhooks my bra. "You're so beautiful, Kiara," he tells me as he takes off his own shirt. He rolls onto his side and pulls me down next to him. We kiss passionately, our tongues dancing together as we hold each other close.

I reach for Paul's belt, and he stops me again. "We're taking it slowly... remember?" he whispers into my ear. "I just want to lay here for a minute, and enjoy the feeling of your bare skin against mine."

He kisses me again, and I wrap my arms around his torso. His smooth chest moves against mine as we breathe in unison, and I lose myself in the emotions of the moment. We continue kissing softly for what seems like both a second and a lifetime. Involuntarily, I start pushing my hips into him once more.

"All right," Paul says, grinning as he pulls away from me. "I can take a hint." He loosens his belt and pulls off his jeans before sliding my pants down my legs. I part my legs and reach for his hips, but he has other ideas.

"You know that a good chef always has to taste what he's working with," he whispers before his head disappears between my legs. I feel his tongue lash against my clit, and I cry out in passion.

"Oh, Paul..." I moan. "Oh, baby... just like that." My eyes roll back in my head as he increases the pressure of his tongue. He slips one finger inside me, and it sends me over the edge. My body spasms and explodes in ecstasy. Paul leaves a trail of kisses from my hip to my earlobe.

"Did that feel good, baby?" he asks me coyly.

"So good," I moan happily. "Would you like me to return the favor?"

He shakes his head. "I'm aching to be inside you," he whispers.

"Then let me offer you some relief." I push him onto his back and climb on top of him. As I lower myself onto his throbbing prick, he reaches up and massages my breasts. I slide down onto him and then remain still for a moment as my pussy stretches to accommodate him.

"You're so tight, baby," he moans. "You feel so good."

I slowly begin moving my hips in wide, clockwise circles. I feel his cock hit every inch of me, and my juices start flowing again.

"You're so wet... god, Kiara, you're so perfect." He sits up and bends his knees. I lean back on his legs and plant my feet on the bed behind him. We hold each other tightly and rock together, slowly at first and then with more urgency. The position we're in puts constant pressure on my G-spot, and I know my second orgasm is imminent.

"I'm going to come again," I warn him.

"Come for me, baby," he whispers in my ear. He nibbles my earlobe and I grip his cock tightly with my internal muscles. We come together quietly with heavy breaths.

We remain locked together long after our orgasms subside. Paul stares lovingly into my eyes. "I've never felt this way before," he confesses.

"I feel the same way," I tell him. I feel a cramp in my thigh and I cringe.

"Are you all right?" he asks, his voice full of concern.

"Leg cramp," I explain.

He smiles back at me… we untangle our bodies and fall asleep in each other's arms.

# Chapter Twelve

I feel soft lips on my face and wake to find Paul lying next to me. His hair is wet, and he smells like soap and aftershave.

"How long have you been awake?" I ask as I stretch.

"About twenty minutes. Coffee is ready, when you want some."

"You should have woken me up before you took a shower. I'd have joined you." Paul's cleanliness emphasizes the fact that I still smell like a kitchen.

"Why don't you enjoy one on your own?" he suggests. "There's a boutique down the street. I can run out and grab you some fresh clothes."

"You'd do that for me?" I ask.

"Kiara, I'd do anything for you," he says.

"Then that sounds like a plan. But don't spend too much money," I insist.

"My robe is hanging on the bathroom door," he tells me. "If I'm not back by the time you get out, feel free to put it on... or don't," he adds with a seductive grin. He helps me off of the bed and we walk hand in hand down the hallway. I stop at the bathroom while he continues on.

Paul's entire apartment is sleek and modern. The shower is a walk-in, with beautiful glass-blocked walls. I turn on the hot water and step into the steam, careful not to let the water touch my skin. My muscles are sore and the steam helps them relax. After a few minutes, I add cold water to the hot and let the spray fall over my body. I am delighted as I survey the products on the shelf of the shower. Paul has three types of expensive, salon-brand shampoos but not one bottle of conditioner. I grab a bottle and wash my hair, knowing that I'm going to have a hard time brushing out the tangles.

I wonder if it's too soon for me to bring some stuff over. Conditioner, a curling iron... maybe some pajamas. Normally, I'd never consider moving stuff in to a man's home so soon, but I'm certain Paul is different. He's gone to buy me a new outfit. I don't think he'll freak out at the sight of my toothbrush.

The water begins to cool so I step out of the shower and dry myself with a fluffy towel. I eye Paul's Jacuzzi and decide that we definitely need to have some fun in it. As I wrap my hair in a towel, Paul's doorbell rings. I wrap myself in his bathrobe and step into the hallway. He must have forgotten his key, I think. I'm proved wrong when I hear the door open.

"Jenny?" I hear him say. "What's wrong?"

"Oh, Paul!" she cries. "I'm so sorry to bother you. I know it's early, but I didn't know where else to go. I just got off the phone with my parents, and they won't help me. They said I've disgraced the family, and they never want to see me again."

"It's okay," he assures her. "Come in and have a seat. Tell me what's happened. What could you have possibly done for your parents to say something like that?"

Part of me wants to join them and offer my friend comfort, but my instincts tell me that that would be a mistake. Instead, I move closer to the living room, but keep myself hidden from their sight.

"It's not something I did, Paul," she sobs. "It's something WE did..."

It's quiet for several moments and dread fills my body.

"You don't mean...?" Paul begins. "But we used protection, Jenny," he says softly.

"I know we did, but I'm knocked up anyway. I've been feeling rotten for the last couple of weeks, but I thought it was just the stress of the job. I haven't been sleeping well either. Last night, I realized my period was late, so I bought a test. I don't want this to be your problem, Paul... I know you're with Kiara, I know that I mean nothing to you..." The rest of her words are lost in her sobs.

"Jenny, I don't mean to sound insensitive, but are you sure the baby is mine?" Paul asks softly. My heart drops to my stomach when I hear the word 'baby'.

"I'm sure," she says, sobbing even louder.

"All right, all right," he says soothingly. "Just calm down. However you want to handle this, I'll help you," he tells her. "Kiara?" he calls out, startling me. "You can come out of the hallway. We all have a lot to talk about."

*-To be continued in Book 2-*

If you enjoyed this title, I would appreciate your leaving a review of the book. Good reviews encourage an author to write as well as help books to sell. Good reviews can be just a few short sentences describing what you liked about the book without having a spoiler. If you could spend 30 seconds writing a review, I would appreciate it: you can review this title right now at your favorite retailer.

Here is a preview of the **next story** you may also enjoy:

"**HOW LONG** on the spot prawns, Chef Kiara?" Robbs asks me with mock reverence from across the kitchen. Two months have passed since I was awarded the apprentice position at Fission. Paul Weston stayed out of the decision. No one was able to outright accuse him of being biased and giving the job to his girlfriend, but the rumors are swirling. The rumors about how I landed my job are the least of my problems, though. Paul and Jenny's upcoming arrival is what really has everyone talking around here.

Every time I think of that fateful morning at Paul's appointment, I'm overwhelmed with the same sick feeling in the pit of my stomach. When Paul called me out of the hallway that morning, Jenny bawled and apologized over and over again. She even offered to get rid of the baby, but Paul and I were against it. Paul had immediately insisted an abortion wasn't an option. I agreed with him, but I still can't wrap my head around the idea that in roughly six months, my boyfriend will have a child with another woman. This wasn't supposed to happen, and I'm helpless to do anything about it.

When the apprenticeship contest ended, Jenny left Fission. It's easier for me to deal with her now that I don't see her every day. Paul spent a lot of time reassuring me that I'm the woman he loves, but a part of me doesn't trust him. Family is important to Paul… he'll want to be a hands-on type of dad, and being with Jenny would make that possible.

A year ago, I'd have never been in this position. The situation unfolding before me is a perfect example of why I never let anyone through my walls. But there is something about Paul that made me drop my guard. I am in love with him, and if this baby is going to be a part of his life then I guess it'll be a part of mine, too. I just hope Jenny keeps a lid on all of the 'baby mama drama.'

"Chef?" Robbs calls loudly and brings my focus back to the present.

"Prawns will be up in three," I tell him.

Never having to put up with Robbs Martin again was what I'd been most looking forward to at the end of the apprenticeship competition. But two days before the contest was over, Paul's prep cook Ernesto gave his notice. Ernesto and his wife had just given birth, and he'd been offered a better paying job that would allow him more time off with his family. Paul was overwhelmed and had no time or patience to interview for a new hire. Before the results of the competition were announced, he opened the prep cook position for one of the runners up. Jenny had already decided to leave Fission and take some time to decide what she really wants to do. Robbs was awarded the job by default. I'd expected the bitchy attitude he'd had during the contest to carry over into his new job, but so far he's actually been pleasant to work with. He shows up on time, he helps the other chefs once his tasks are finished, and he makes friendly conversation while doing so. I'm enjoying his new work attitude, but I still don't trust him any farther than I can throw him. Robbs already showed me his true colors, and I don't give people second chances... except for Paul, that is.

I pull the prawns from the grill, plate them, and carry them to Robbs' station. He sets them next to the vegetables he's already prepped for tonight's seafood chowder.

"Did you toss the shells and tails into the stock pot?" Robbs asks me, as if I don't know what I'm doing.

"Of course I did," I answer politely. I can't stand the guy, but I'm not going to give him the satisfaction of letting him get to me.

"Thanks, Chef," he says with a fake smile.

I nod at him and return to my station. I'm doing an appetizer special tonight, and I need to get everything prepped. I prefer to do my own knife work, instead of relying on Robbs. *I have plenty of time for prep work. It's kind of hard to be a chef's apprentice when the chef is never here...*

The toll Jenny's pregnancy took on my job was even harder than the toll it was taking on my personal life. Paul is constantly leaving work to go to doctor's appointments or to shop for cribs. Once he left just because Jenny was craving cheese soup from Mamma's Kettle and was too tired to leave her apartment to pick it up. I had a lot of freedom in the kitchen, but I fought for *the job to learn from Paul, not to cover* for him.

I can't let myself drown in frustration. Not when a lot of work needs to be done. I fill three stock pots with water and set them to boil on the stove. To one I add cumin, cinnamon, and chili powder. The second gets saffron and kefir limes, while the third is seasoned with basil and rosemary. The pots begin to boil, so I toss a handful of salt into each, add my rice, and carefully replace the lids. I turn off the burners and turn my attention to my proteins. I'm making a sushi trio inspired by different areas of the world. I want to do a marinated beef tartar for the Latin roll, but I'm still torn between a couple of different fish for the Indian and the Mediterranean. I need to consider our stock of each of the fish, so I set off for the walk-in cooler.

"Chef Kiara?" a voice calls from behind me. I turn and see Megan, one of the hostesses, standing in the kitchen doorway.

"What is it now?" I groan.

If you enjoyed this sample then look for **Fifty Recipes For Disaster - Book 2**.


Here is a preview of **another story** you may enjoy:

**Secrets Revealed: Obsessed Bounty Hunter New Adult Romance Series, Book 1**

**JACQUI SCHNEIDER** awoke with a sudden start, the unfamiliarity of her surroundings sending waves of panic sweeping all through her body. Her head whipped frantically from side to side as her eyes swept across the shadowy interior.

She could see the white sheer curtain drawn across the glass window. The sky outside the window had a purplish hue, indicating the first blush of dawn. A console table just below the window held a tray with a thermos bottle and a cup and saucer set neatly stacked beside it. A beige telephone and a digital clock with the time displayed as 4:27 a.m. rested on the other side of the console table. She recognized her clothes as they lay strewn on the floor. Her high-heeled shoes and purse lay in a pile near the door.

She was in a hotel room. As awareness took over, Jacqui was glad her sudden movement did not disturb the sleeping form beside her. She glanced at the figure snoring softly and saw his hand reach out for her. He stirred, breathing deeply, and then resumed his sleep. Jacqui hoped he would not notice the empty space beside him as she tiptoed silently out of bed and gathered her clothes from the floor.

Jacqui wanted to leave the hotel before the man woke up. Things were less complicated that way. She couldn't even remember his name. Was it John… or Jack… or Jim…?

Jacqui didn't really care. It was strictly sexual. She had no intention of ever seeing him again. He was just a random guy she had picked up in the hotel bar last night. The guys were always the same. Non-threatening, married, from out of town, and only out to have a good time. A few made a play of removing their wedding rings. But Jacqui could always spot the telltale lighter skin tone where the ring used to be.

This suited Jacqui just fine. It wasn't a good idea to hook up with someone local. She always made sure the guy was at the hotel for a convention, or just an overnight stay. She usually spotted them because of the name tag pinned over their breast pocket. She'd sit in the bar with her drink, until someone struck up a conversation or offered her a drink.

Jacqui was very hard not to notice. She was tall and lithe and had full breasts, milky white skin, and a nice round ass. She had sparkling green eyes, high cheekbones and luscious lips, topped by chestnut brown hair that fell softly to her shoulders; she attracted instant attention.

And this guy…Jim…Jacqui suddenly remembered, was no different. He made a beeline for her as soon as he spotted her at the bar.

"Hi, my name's Jim… I hope you don't mind the intrusion…" Jacqui remembered him saying. "But it looks like your glass needs a refill."

Jacqui gave him a smile. It was the standard pickup line. He didn't know she already pegged him through the glass mirrors lining the liquor cabinet of the bar. He was going to be "it" for tonight.

"Are you staying in this hotel?" Jim asked, signaling the bartender for another shot of brandy for her.

"No…" Jacqui answered.

"Are you waiting for someone…?" Jim asked.

Jacqui could read the expectant look in his eyes, and this was usually her cue. If she didn't like what she saw or if she had second thoughts about her safety, she'd say… "Yes, I'm just waiting for my boyfriend to pick me up…" Or offer some other lame excuse.

But she had liked what she saw. Jim was tall, good-looking and neatly dressed. And he had a ring on his finger.

"No…" Jacqui answered and gave him a flirty smile. "My name is Nina…" she added.

Yes, she would be a horny Nina tonight, or Glenna, or Linda. It didn't really matter. She just wanted to get laid. And tonight, Jim was it.

Jacqui could predict how the next hour would play out. Jim will tell her his life story as he kept filling up her glass hoping to get her drunk enough so she would be pliant when he made his move. The thought almost made Jacqui laugh. The poor guy didn't know that was exactly her plan.

"You've hardly told me anything about yourself, Nina…" Jim complained playfully, as his hand dropped down to her knee.

"There's really nothing to tell…I'm just a girl hoping to get lucky tonight…" Jacqui whispered seductively in his ear.

His hand moved a little further up her skirt as Jacqui opened her legs a little wider to allow him to feel her crotch through her sheer stockings.

Jim's eyes opened wide in surprise as he felt the heat emanating through the silk.

"Why don't we finish this conversation upstairs in my room?" Jim asked.

Jacqui nodded her head in reply as her bosom heaved in anticipation. This was the reason she was here tonight. This guy, Jim, would make her forget even for just a few hours, those thoughts and images that constantly lurked in her psyche, tormenting her. When they came uninvited, Jacqui knew what would make her forget. Sex.

Jacqui sashayed her way out of the bar ahead of him. She wanted him to see her firm ass, tapered waist, and long slim legs. It was hard to ignore the looks from other men that followed her and this aroused her even more. She made her way out and straight into the banks of elevators.

Jim could hardly contain his excitement. His erection was bulging through his pants.

As soon as the bedroom door closed behind them, Jacqui dropped down on her knees and unzipped his pants. She grabbed hold of his cock. She spit down on it as her hands feverishly stroked it. Jim was hardly out of his pants before Jacqui had him inside her mouth.

Jim threw back his head in arousal. He was stunned at the ferocity with which Jacqui moved her head back and forth, her saliva leaving his shaft red and glistening. Jacqui toyed with the head of his cock and tasted the sweet dew that signaled that he would cum prematurely if she didn't slow down.

And Jim didn't want to cum just yet. He had plans of sucking and tasting every inch of her. He would fuck her hard, until the tension building inside his body became unbearable, and then he would blow his load in her mouth.

He pulled her up and began to unhook her bra. Jacqui's face was wild with anticipation as she shimmied out of her clothes and stockings. A slight sweat broke out in her armpits. Her boobs swelled as Jim groped one breast with his hand and twirled his thumb and forefinger around the sensitive nipple. Using his mouth, he sucked on the other nipple. Jacqui arched her back in pleasure as waves of ice and fire shot straight through to her groin.

Jim continued sucking her breast and nibbling her nipple with his teeth. His other hand traveled down her flat stomach. He stopped just below her mound, feeling the coarse pubes that covered her vagina. Using his fingers to separate the lips, he caressed her clit and discovered just how wet and aroused she was. Jim stroked her clit repeatedly. He slid in another finger, adding pressure with every stroke. He could feel the inner muscles of her vagina tightening each time his hand brushed against her swollen clitoris. Jacqui closed her eyes and moaned her pleasure. Getting fingered felt really good.

But Jacqui knew she wanted more than his fingers. Pulling him along, she lay back against the bed and opened her thighs. Her pussy was slick with her own juice.

"Do you like what you see?" she whispered up at him as Jim nodded.

"Eat me. Show me what your tongue can do…" she whispered huskily as she caressed herself to arouse him.

Jacqui grabbed her knees and spread her legs even wider for him, leaning her head back against the pillow. Her invitation was obvious, insistent.

Jim scrambled up the bed, his erect penis bouncing with the movement. Then he knelt down between her legs, enthralled with the red-hot pussy before him. He lowered his head as his hands separated the lips of her vagina, exposing the engorged clit. He flicked his tongue against it as Jacqui's body heaved with pleasure. He flicked repeatedly; mesmerized by the guttural sounds emanating from Jacqui's mouth each time his rough tongue made contact with the sensitive skin.

She began to moan as he went faster and faster until finally she couldn't take it anymore. She wanted to feel his cock inside her.

Jim positioned himself on top of her. He used his elbows to steady himself as his cock searched for her vagina's opening. Jacqui savored the feeling of the velvety skin of his cock rubbing against the slick wetness of her clit. Jim rammed himself inside her. And then he drew back until the head of his cock was barely past the opening of her vaginal wall. Then he rammed into her once again, filling her completely.

If you enjoyed this sample then look for **Secrets Revealed: Obsessed Bounty Hunter New Adult Romance Series, Book 1**.

Here is a preview of **another story** you may enjoy:

**KRISTIE LOOKED** at the sky as she pulled up in front of the casino. The air was chilly and the clouds were dark and threatening snow, which was the last thing Kristie felt like dealing with. She had been in her car for over ten hours, driving home from college for the holidays. Her back was sore and her legs needed to be stretched out. She wanted a hot bath in a Jacuzzi tub. She'd settle for a hot tub. But who was she kidding? There was no hot tub to be found at her parents' house and trying to have a hot bath without being interrupted was almost impossible.

Kristie had approached the holidays with an ever-growing sense of dread. It wasn't that she didn't want to see her mother, but every time she came home, it was like being suffocated. Her hometown had held more appeal for her when she was younger, back when her father was alive. Since he'd died and her mother had gotten remarried last year, Kristie had delayed going home at all. She had only met her step-father in passing and hadn't met his nephew, who he tried to raise on his own.

Kristie had saved up to stay at a hotel the entire break. It had made the most sense to her. It would cause the least amount of stress during her stay and give her space when she needed it. But when she had mentioned this to her mother, there was no way to mistake the sadness in her mother's voice for anything else. Knowing she was upsetting her mother by refusing to stay at home with her new family, Kristie had cancelled the reservation and agreed to stay at her mother's house instead.

She looked up at the casino where her mother had worked the last five years. Her mother worked in the back offices, far away from the lights from the slot machines and the sounds of people winning money. The casino was a little run down but brought in a steady stream of people who could afford the middle-level slots and risks it provided in a town that was mostly quiet.

The stale smell of cigarettes and alcohol hit Kristie in the face as she stepped inside. She looked around, seeing if anything had changed since the last time she had been here. Nothing jumped out of her. A few of the slots seemed to have been upgraded, but the carpet was still worn down and dirty and the place had an air of despair that made Kristie's skin crawl. She had never been to Las Vegas, but she imagined that the casinos there weren't as depressing.

Kristie made her way to the back and asked for her mother through the grate where an attendant was standing, looking at her cellphone. The woman went off to find her mother, and Kristie was soon ushered into the back offices. The casino décor quickly ended back here. Her mother's small office was near the back, shoved in a corner. The door was ajar, and Kristie peeked her head in.

Her mother was looking at the computer, squinting through her glasses to whatever was on the screen. When Kristie knocked on the door gently, her mother looked up and smiled. Kristie was startled to see she was going gray. The last time she had seen her mother, she had been a brunette. It was odd to see age creeping up on her. She came over to her and hugged her tightly.

"It's so nice to see you again."

"You, too, Mom."

Her mom urged her to sit down as she sat across from her at her desk. It made Kristie feel odd, as if she was interviewing to be her mother's daughter. Her mom didn't seem to notice, however, and smiled again. They made small talk for a while, mostly talking about Kristie's experiences at college. Kristie felt tired. She knew her mom meant well, but she really wanted to go home and nap. She was only here to get the address to her mom's new place.

"How are things with Lionel?" Kristie finally asked, feeling as if she didn't bring up her mom's new husband, she would never get out of the tiny office.

Her mom seemed to relax now that Kristie had brought him up, "He's great. Really, we're just wonderful. There are some issues, though…"

"Like what?"

"Well, it's actually one of the reasons that we wanted you to stay with us instead of a hotel. See, Lionel's nephew, Gray, is a bit of a handful. Lionel still feels responsible for him since he became his legal guardian when Gray was just a little boy."

Kristie wasn't following, "Okay…"

"He tends to run on the wrong side of the law, and we thought it'd be so great if you two could meet and maybe hang out."

The words hung in the air. Kristie felt a twinge of annoyance. She had thought her mother wanted her at the house because she had missed her, not because she wanted her to play nice with her new step-father's nephew. They weren't in grade school anymore. Trying to change someone set in their ways by sticking them with a goody-goody was a useless attempt.

Kristie took a deep breath and held it for a few seconds, letting the air out slowly. Her mother watched, a worried expression on her face.

"What do you want me to do with him?" Kristie finally asked.

Her mom, taking the fact that Kristie hadn't said no as a good sign, started to ramble. "Well, maybe just hang out with him. Show him what you do for fun. Maybe you two can go to the movies or something."

Kristie raised an eyebrow, "Go to the movies? What does this guy do for fun anyway that has you two so stressed out?"

Her mom avoided her stare and sighed, looking tired. "He runs with a bad crowd and doesn't like to listen. He's a good kid though. He's just lost."

"And you think I can fix him?"

"It wouldn't hurt to try, would it, Kristie? For me?"

Kristie sighed and nodded in agreement. How could she say no to her mother? She would always wish that her mother hadn't gotten remarried, but she didn't want her mom to be unhappy either. Her mom got up and walked over to her, hugging her tightly. Her mother's hugs had always reminded Kristie of being a little kid, outside playing till the sun set and running back inside for dinner. Back when her father was alive. Kristie shut her eyes tightly, willing the memories to leave her. She didn't want to think about her father right now.

Her mom finally pulled away and looked at her, smiling, "We'll have to really talk, you know, all about college and everything."

"Yeah, of course."

Her mom's eyes swept down her quickly, so fast that if Kristie wasn't used to it, she never would have picked up on it. She steeled herself.

"Maybe you and Gray can go to the gym. It'd get him out of the house and you could lose a few pounds at the same time," her mom said cheerfully.

Kristie mumbled in agreement and gave her mother one last hug before leaving the office. She should have known that there wasn't going to be any way in hell that her mother would have let an entire conversation go without making some sort of remark to her about her weight.

As she trudged through the casino, her mood lowered with every step. She regretted coming here for the holidays. Before her, they spread out in a bleak landscape. Dealing with her mother's 'helpful advice' in regards to her weight, and trying to show her loser relative by marriage around town. At the very least, she should have kept the hotel reservation.

Kristie dragged out the drive toward Lionel's house. Her mother had given her the address and it was close to the casino. A ten-minute drive didn't seem like enough time to prepare for whatever she was going to walk into. As she turned down the street where her mom's new house was, she found herself taking a deep breath. The first time, she just drove past the house. It was non-descript and had nothing of worth showing that made Kristie even notice it. Her mom had stopped gardening after her father died, and the front yard of this house was plain and dull.

Kristie pulled into the driveway. The garage door was open and a man was underneath a truck, working on it. She could only see his feet. Kristie got out of her car, grabbing her bags, and looked inside the garage. The man didn't look up when she shut the door of her car.

"Hello?" Kristie called out toward the man under the truck.

He didn't answer. Heavy metal was blasting out of a stereo nearby, but it was such an old stereo that the music sounded tinny. Kristie called out again, but the man still didn't answer. She knew that he heard her because he stopped working at one point and went still before resuming. She hoped this wasn't Lionel, because the guy was an asshole. *Probably his fantastic nephew.*

Kristie trudged toward the front door, leaving the other guy behind. What a fantastic trip this was going to be.

If you enjoyed this sample then look for **Devil's Advocate: A BBW MC New Adult Romance Series - Book 1**.

# Other Books by Carla Coxwell

- Star Bright New Adult Romance Series (This series follows "Fifty Recipes For Disaster New Adult Romance Series")

- Torrid Exposure New Adult Romance Series

- Devil's Advocate BBW MC New Adult Romance Series

- Obsessed Bounty Hunter Romance Series


Get the latest update on new releases from the author at:

https://www.carlacoxwell.com/newsletter

# About the Author - Carla Coxwell

Carla has always been a fan of romance novels. To augment what she made waiting on tables to help her way through college, Carla also did some freelance work in the romance genre.

Now she enjoys living vicariously through her characters in her New Adult Romance books.

# Connect with Carla Coxwell

I really appreciate you reading my book!  Here are my social media coordinates:

Friend me on Facebook:
https://www.facebook.com/CarlaCoxwell/

Follow me on Twitter: https://twitter.com/carlacoxwell

Check me out on Goodreads:
https://www.goodreads.com/author/show/10691544.Carla_Coxwell

Subscribe to my newsletter:
https://www.carlacoxwell.com/newsletter/

Visit my website: https://www.carlacoxwell.com/